LEGENDS: BEN

Legends of Fire Creek Series
Book Four

BY SHELLEY JUSTICE

COPYRIGHT

DEDICATION

To my beautiful Ally, who is living her love story – one more beautiful than anything I could write. You are my pride and joy, my best friend, and my strong encourager. I love you more than you ever know, and I'm excited to see how your future unfolds with your Prince Charming. Just remember, even when you become a married woman, even when you're old and gray, you will always be my baby girl.

ABOUT THIS BOOK

CHARLOTTE

Charlotte lives a quiet, monotonous life. Her days remain the same. Her dreams are ignored. It's the way it has to be for her to stay invisible. Calling attention to herself could spell her death. It's a risk she won't take, but that doesn't stop her from longing for more.

BEN

Ben has watched his brothers find love, but it's not in the cards for him. His life as a Legend is demanding enough, and he never knows what awaits him from day to day. A new case takes him to a small town where he meets the mysterious Charlotte. The beautiful woman is hiding something — something that has her terrified.

Charlotte doesn't trust people easily, but Ben can't walk away from someone in trouble. When the Legend brings danger to Charlotte instead of rescuing her from it, he's faced with the toughest case of his life — one that could rip away the love he never thought he'd have.

Meet the
LEGENDS OF FIRE CREEK

They were once wayward boys until they were taken under the wing of the original Legend. They grew under his tutelage to become vigilantes who look after those who aren't able to help themselves. They are loners thrown together in an unconventional family, living with secrets that shaped them into the men they've become. It's the life they've chosen — until they meet the women who show them what it means to be loved and accepted for who they are.

CHAPTER ONE

Ben Weston was already making his way to the front door of his house before he heard the short knock against the wood. Swinging the door open, he felt a powerful wind blow past him into his home. He thought the gust sounded a lot like his five-year-old nephew Jax, but the force moved too fast for him to be sure.

"Jax Moore, stop running and show some manners, or you can forget about a bedtime story tonight."

Reagan Moore stepped into Ben's house, her expression stern as she yelled after her son. Her shiny dark hair was pulled into a ponytail, which swung against her back when she moved. Her angular features bore no makeup, but her high cheekbones and wide eyes needed no enhancement. Even dressed in an oversized sweatshirt and leggings, Reagan was breathtaking, far too pretty to saddle to his oldest brother Jackson, but he and the rest of their family were glad she was. Since coming into their lives, Reagan was a fixture they wondered how they ever lived without.

And the fact that she was a good mother to his nephew only gave Ben one more reason to adore his sister-in-law.

Jax paused only for a second in his frantic search of Ben's house. The six-year-old had Reagan's dark eyes but Jackson's coloring and stocky build. Even at his young age, Jax showed signs of being tall and husky like his father. He had the wherewithal to look sheepish as he apologized for his lack of manners.

"Sorry, Uncle Ben. Hi. Where is he? I don't see him. I can take care of him, Uncle Ben. I really can. Is he here?" Jax spoke with the same exuberance he had with doing anything. The little bundle of energy may look just like Ben's brother, but Jax's temperament was all his own.

Reagan sighed as she looked up at Ben in resignation. "I should never have told him why we were coming. He's been talking about Ziggy nonstop since he got up this morning."

Ben chuckled. "You can't blame him for being excited. He's been wanting a pet since he was old enough to say the word. I wish you'd let us get him one."

Her stare turned into a glare. "No way. That boy can barely concentrate long enough to make it through the school day. I won't have him forgetting to feed his pet or take it outside to do its business. He needs to be a little older before we add any animals to our household."

"Here he is!" Jax shouted. "I found him!"

The little boy appeared from the back of the house, staggering under the weight of a massive cat. Its hind legs and tail trailed along the floor since the Maine coon cat was as big, if not bigger than, the little boy. To the cat's credit, it didn't seem to mind that Jax dragged it from room to room.

Reagan called after him. "Jax, put Ziggy down gently before you drop and hurt him."

"Okay." Jax attempted to lower the cat to the ground, and the cat helped him out by wiggling out of his arms until it landed on all fours.

"I still can't believe you adopted that beast," Reagan murmured.

Ziggy walked over to rub against Ben's legs, purring as it moved. Ben's hand stroked the thick fur, a pretty blend of white and gray unlike any cat he'd ever seen.

"Sometimes I can't either," he admitted.

Ben ran the Fire Creek Hardware Store, and he'd been working the front counter one afternoon when a customer came in asking to post a notice about a litter of Main coon cats he was giving away. Ben had been surprised when she said she wasn't selling the expensive breed. She only wanted to find the kittens good homes. Without knowing anything about the breed, Ben agreed to take one and let his customer choose which. That's when Ziggy came into his life.

He'd considered himself a dog person until he learned more about the cat. With his travel schedule and unpredictable personal life, the cat proved to be a decent companion. Ziggy was low-maintenance and even-tempered. When Ben had to be gone for more than a day or two, his family checked on the furball occasionally, and the rest of the time, Ziggy was content to keep to himself.

"I appreciate you checking in on Ziggy for me while I'm gone."

Reagan watched Jax drag one of the cat's toys along the floor and then laugh when the cat pounced on it.

"No worries. Melody told me he was easy going, so I figured this would be a good lesson in responsibility for Jax."

Melody was married to his brother Luke and was Ziggy's regular pet sitter. But she'd woken that morning to find a sick child. His nephew Dylan was running a fever, so Melody was at the pediatrician with her son. He didn't hesitate to reassure her he'd find someone to care for Ziggy while he was out of town, but Melody had already reached out to Reagan to help out.

Ben pointed toward the kitchen. "Let me show you where I keep Ziggy's food."

Quickly explaining the workings of the automatic feeder that kept Ziggy's water and food bowl full, he also showed her where the bags of his food were kept. Depending on how long he'd be gone on his trip, Reagan may have to replenish the feeder, and he didn't want her having to search for anything. He also showed her how to empty the waste from the self-cleaning litter box.

"Too bad they don't make all of this automatic stuff for babies. It sure would have come in handy when Jax was born," she mumbled.

Ben laughed. "Speaking of baby, you hear anything from Mel about Dylan?"

"Yeah, the doctor said it's nothing serious. A virus of some kind that'll run its course."

Ben stood behind the kitchen island, leaning against the sink as they talked. Reagan bent at the waist to rest her crossed arms on the counter in front of him. Her dark eyes studied him intently, and he waited for her to say whatever was on her mind.

"How are *you* doing?"

He smirked. "I'm good. How are you?"

She scowled. "Be serious. I know how cases involving children twist you boys into knots."

Ben and his brothers had been known as *the boys* since they came to live with their mentor, English Barlowe. Even now that they were grown men, they couldn't escape the moniker given by the folks in their hometown of Fire Creek, Alabama. Long ago they had learned not to care about the nickname, but escaping the effects of their pasts wasn't as easy. They all came to English from broken homes, bringing more baggage than a bachelor like English would want to take on.

But take them in English did, and he taught them how to be men, how to fight for the underdog, and how to never let anyone take advantage of them. As a former operative for the Central Intelligence Agency known as Legend, English's work wrecked his attempt at being a husband and father, and he walked away from his family then to protect them from any blowback from his work.

He atoned for his choice when he left the CIA by using what

he learned as Legend to help those who couldn't find help through traditional means. As the boys became old enough to understand English's off-the-radar work, they joined him as the next generation of Legends. Ben and his brothers were business owners, but they routinely accepted cases involving people who needed help, sometimes individually and sometimes as a team.

When the cases involved children, it was hard for Ben and his brothers not to be reminded of their own difficult upbringings. They'd learned to push their emotions deep down where they didn't affect their work, but those memories were hard to escape.

"I'm fine, Ray. And if I'm not, I know who to call. At this point, I'm not sure there's even a case here. I figure I'll go to Georgia for a few days, sort it all out, and be back before you have a chance to miss me."

Reagan sighed. "Our client is very convincing, and I don't know why, but I believe she's right. Something is off about the boy and his father. If the man is abusing his son, I hope you bury him."

Ben appreciated the heat behind her words. "I'll be thorough. I'll keep you posted on my progress. You just watch my cat and keep my brothers out of trouble."

Reagan rolled her eyes. "Like that's even possible. But at least I have help now since Luke and Easton have married Mel and Bailee. Speaking of marriage, I met someone the other day who I think would be perfect for you."

Ben narrowed his eyes. "You sure it's murder mysteries you write and not those cheesy romance novels? It seems like you always have love and matchmaking on the brain."

In addition to managing the incoming requests for the Legends' help, Reagan was also a successful author of intriguing whodunits which kept readers on their toes and guessing until the very end.

Reagan straightened her posture and pointed an accusing finger in his direction. "I'll have you know that many of those romance novels are very well written and contribute to a multi-million-dollar industry. So check yourself before you call them cheesy. And there's nothing wrong with a little romance. Your brothers found it. I think you're past due to find yours."

His sister-in-law had a point. He and his brothers never imagined settling down with families of their own, but then Jackson met and married Reagan. Luke found happiness with Melody, and Easton fell in love with Bailee. He even suspected English was starting to romance their family friend, Becky Lathan, who was one of the people English helped back in the day.

But romance wasn't for Ben. He was content with the life he had. He was close with his family, and his nephews filled any need he had for kids. His freedom was something he treasured. He answered to no one and did just what he wanted. There was something to the semi-solitary life, and he wasn't willing to trade it in for something else, even if he was happy to see his brothers start families.

"I appreciate your concern, but I have no interest in falling in love. And I can find my own dates. I'm too busy right now for more than that, so even if I agreed to let you set me up, I would only be wasting your friend's time."

Reagan sighed. "You know I love you, Bear. You deserve someone who appreciates the kind of guy you are."

He smiled at her use of the nickname she gave him because of his considerable size. "What kind of guy am I?"

"Successful. Kind. Hot. You know, all the things," she answered nonchalantly as Jax came tearing through the room with Ziggy hot on his heels.

"Jax Moore, stop running through the house!"

"Yes, ma'am," the little boy called, slowing his pace to a half-walk, half-run.

Reagan shook her head as if saying without words that her son was hopeless. "If I had half of his energy, I could take over the world."

Ben chuckled. "Like you couldn't do that anyway."

She pursed her lips as if considering Ben's remark. "Very true. Anyway, time to go, Jax!"

"Aww, Momma, can't I play with Ziggy a little longer?"

"Nope. Uncle Ben has to get going, but we'll be back later to check on Ziggy. You can play with him then."

"Okay. Bye, Ziggy." Jax enveloped the cat in a hug, and Ben tried not to laugh at how Ziggy looked ready to run. Jax then hurried over to wrap his arms around Ben's legs. "Bye, Uncle Ben. Be safe."

The two words were something his family had gotten into the habit of saying to each other, and the words coming from his nephew tugged at his heart. He lifted Jax into his arms to hug him back.

"Thanks, buddy. You be good and help out your momma."

"Okay." Jax wiggled out of his uncle's arms. Ben lowered him gently to the floor and watched him run ahead to the door.

Ben stopped them before they stepped outside. "So who's the friend you wanted to set me up with?"

Thinking she had him on the hook, Reagan's eyes lit up. "She's the new librarian. I met her when Jax went to a story time the town library was having. She's very cute. Petite. Sweet. Has a great sense of humor."

"I know. I've dated her already."

Reagan blinked in surprise. "You did?"

Ben nodded. "Not long after she moved to town. We went out to dinner twice. She's pretty and very nice. But she smacks her lips while she eats because she chews with her mouth open."

He knew the trait was a particular pet peeve of his sister-in-law, so he waited for her to digest the information.

"Enough said. Come on, Jax."

Ben waved after them as they headed to the car. He was pleased that he had effectively shut down Reagan's matchmaking for now. He had a feeling the reprieve wouldn't last long, but he wouldn't worry about it. He had a case which needed his attention.

He went to grab his bag holding enough clothes and essentials for a few days away from home. He needed to get on the road if he was to make his meeting with the client — a school teacher who suspected a little boy in her class of being abused by his single father. The authorities investigated and determined there wasn't enough evidence to prove abuse, but the teacher felt certain something was wrong. She was worried for her student, and he suspected the teacher tugged at Reagan's heartstrings with her story. As the mother to a son, Reagan didn't have it in her to dismiss the teacher's concern as quickly as local law enforcement had.

After Reagan briefed him on the case, he wasn't so sure the authorities missed anything. The teacher had been in the game long enough to know the signs of abuse, but Ben already suspected she was wrong in this case. His brother Luke had hacked the system and secured the report on the investigation. After looking it over, Ben discovered the authorities had been thorough.

Deep down, Ben felt they should have turned down the case, but he wasn't about to argue the point with Reagan. If she wanted him to look into it, he would sacrifice a few days to satisfy her concerns.

CHAPTER TWO

Charlotte Redding moved the dust cloth over the top of the reservation desk until the surface shone. She repeated the movement on the other furnishings in the motel's lobby until she was satisfied with how everything looked. A glance at the digital clock on the reservation desk showed her she was right on time.

Tossing the cloth on her maid's cart, she removed her plastic gloves and tossed them into a trash bag. She moved over to the coffee station the motel kept stocked for guests and went through the motions of preparing a fresh pot, just as she did every morning.

Charlotte's schedule was routine, and while it was monotonous at times, she appreciated the ease of always knowing what to expect each day. As the only overnight lodging option in Ivy Springs, Georgia, the Skyline Motel stayed surprisingly busy. Motels often had a bad reputation for being less than ideal, but the Skyline was not run down or unsafe. The owner, Nolan Wallace, prided himself on maintaining a quality establishment, and he was particular about many things, such as providing amenities while keeping the nightly rates reasonable.

He also took a chance on hiring Charlotte when she had no experience, no references, and nowhere else to go.

Charlotte started her shift at the motel at seven in the morning with the same tasks every day. She cleaned the common areas, reserving one day for a thorough dusting, one day for cleaning and polishing the floors, and another day for freshening the furniture.

Every day had her cleaning bathrooms, restocking the fruit, drinks, and snacks for the guests, and keeping the coffee pot full.

The coffee wasn't anything special, but for some reason, Wally — as her boss was called by just about everyone who knew him — preferred how she brewed it. Since he was the one who drank most of it, even when they had guests, she was happy to fill the coffee pots during her shift.

Giving guests time to rise or check out, she would refresh any empty rooms, polishing surfaces, disinfecting bathrooms, and changing out linens if needed. Then she did her work in occupied rooms, checking the common areas in between, and would call it a day, only to repeat the process during her next shift.

She'd completed her work in the lobby by the time the coffee finished brewing, filling the lobby with a rich aroma she never tired of. As if on cue, Wally's key turned in the lock at the back, giving him access through his private office. Soon, he appeared behind the reservation desk with a ready smile for her.

"Charlotte! How's my favorite employee this morning?"

Charlotte rolled her eyes at the familiar greeting. He used the same words in some form or fashion every morning she worked. The bar wasn't set very high for the honor of favorite employee. Wally spent the majority of his days at the motel, so he oversaw reservations, billing, and general maintenance. There was a part-time housekeeper who'd been working at the motel since it opened, but since her attitude was sour at best, she and Wally butted heads so much that Charlotte was surprised Wally hadn't fired Betsy.

"Good morning, Wally. Coffee's ready."

"Great. I could use a mug full."

Charlotte smiled as her boss shuffled over to the coffee pot, his favorite mug clean and ready to be used. Wally made her think of a grandpa in a television sitcom. His light brown hair was thinning up top and graying at his temples. His thick mustache was a combination of white and brown hair. She judged him to be in his sixties, and though his frame was trim and fit, he moved as if a touch of arthritis affected his knees. His eyes were the most fascinating — hard as steel when needed, warm and friendly when he saw Charlotte, soft and loving when he was with his longtime girlfriend.

"How's Mona this morning?" she asked about said girlfriend.

"Woke up sick, but dammit, she's going to work anyway. Like there's going to be a rush on the flower shop today if she's not there."

Mona Hillyard owned Ivy Florals and was as much of a workaholic as her boyfriend, but Charlotte had a strong fondness for both. They were her first friends when she came to town, and she trusted them more than anyone in her life right now.

"If you want to check on her later, let me know. I'll man the office for you."

"You don't have to, but I appreciate the offer." Wally blew across the surface of his coffee and took a sip. "Damn, that's good."

"Glad you approve. Anything I need to know before I get started on the rooms?"

"We rented one-fourteen Monday. He paid for several days because he wasn't sure how long he'd be in town. I forget his name, but he put a card on file. He wants us to hold housekeeping services unless he requests them."

Charlotte nodded, not surprised by the guest's preference. Some patrons preferred to maintain their privacy during their stay.

Wally closed the distance between them with a thoughtful expression on his face. "Listen. If the guy makes a request, let me handle it. If it's something I can't do, I'll call Betsy in. Just consider it one room you don't have to worry about while the guy is here."

Charlotte stiffened, panic stealing her breath. She was sure all color drained from her face when Wally suddenly approached her, concern etched in his features.

"No, no, Charlotte. He's not one of them. You're safe. I swear it."

Charlotte's lungs started to burn, and she struggled to regain her breathing. "Are you sure?" Her voice squeaked, and she hated how small and vulnerable she sounded.

"I'm sure. He's working on the construction site in town. The construction company made his reservation, so it's legit."

Charlotte placed a hand to her chest as if to stop her heart from pounding so hard. "Then why do you want me to ignore his room?"

"Because he's a big guy. Dark hair. Kind of quiet. Friendly enough, but I'd be wary of him if I ran into him in a dark alley. I didn't want you to feel uncomfortable around him. And he's a stranger. He might seem like a good guy, but you can't ever tell these days."

Charlotte shook her head, appreciative of how Wally looked out for her. "You had me worried there for a moment. Look, I promise I'll be careful around him, but I'm here to do a job, Wally. You don't have to protect me from every stranger who stays at the motel. I'm sorry I overreacted."

Understanding shone in Wally's eyes. "You didn't overreact. I'm sorry if I scared you. It just seems like you finally feel safe here. I don't want to do anything to change that. Forgive me for being protective of you. Mona and I have grown fond of you, and I can't help wanting to look out for you. Mona says I act like a caveman sometimes, but I don't mean anything by it."

She smiled as she stepped in to hug him. He seemed surprised by her action, but after a moment, he wrapped his arms around her to awkwardly pat her back. Charlotte stepped away from him, affection replacing her fear instantly.

"Thank you for looking out for me. If I feel uncomfortable taking care of the man's requests, I'll let you know. I promise. I should get to work."

Wally pursed his lips as he studied her. "No. Take a break instead. I gave you a scare, so take a moment to collect yourself. Then you can start on the rooms. A few minutes to relax are hardly going to throw you behind on your work."

She nodded. "Okay. Thank you, Wally. I don't know what I'd do without you watching out for me."

The tips of his ears flushed red, and he turned back to the coffee pot. "Go on. Take your break and then get to work."

She smiled as Wally busied himself with topping off the cup of coffee that was neither empty nor cool. Taking pity on him, she headed for the back door he had entered through, throwing one last parting remark over her shoulder.

"You know where to find me if something comes up."

Once outside, Charlotte pulled her thrift store black jacket closer to her body to ward off the chill. Her entire housekeeping uniform was black, which hid any dirt her clothes collected as she cleaned and helped her to blend into the background. Her black shoes were ugly but heavy-soled and offered better support since she was on her feet all day. They cushioned her steps as she moved over the back parking lot to a grassy area on the side. She settled on the bench of a picnic table, letting the cool air sweep over her.

The winter weather had been unpredictable at best. January was halfway over, and the unseasonably warm weather was being shoved to the side by a cold front which chilled the temperatures and added a dampness to the air. Charlotte didn't mind the cooler weather. Something about this time of year produced yearnings for hot cider, pots of homemade soup, and cozy fires.

Her hands balled into fists as she fought against a familiar urge which never really left her. Many people would find this time of year desolate, with the leaves off the trees, the grass dead, wildlife hibernating, and fewer people outside. With her favorite digital camera in her hand, peering through the viewfinder, she found this time of year mysterious, almost romantic, like a secret long hidden and waiting to be discovered.

Capturing the world as she saw it was a passion that ran deep. No matter what she tried, she couldn't squelch it or forget about it. A year had passed since she last held a camera, and she rarely used the camera feature on her cell because snapping even a selfie was a joy she could no longer afford. Her life depended on her leaving that part of her long buried in her past.

She still remembered the day she was forced to walk away from her passion. It was a day she both missed and loathed. It haunted her nightmares and changed her life forever. She wished the memory had faded over time. Her life would be simpler. Well, maybe not simple, but manageable. Hell, not even that. She'd already managed the changes in her life. She'd learned to adapt, to accept the way things had to be. But she still dreamed. She still yearned. She still indulged in *what-ifs*.

Days like today, when she had a hint of her past finding her, reminded her of why she made the choices she had to make. Being a photographer was her joy, but if she had a hope of staying invisible, of remaining hidden, she couldn't risk showing any semblance of the person she once was.

CHAPTER THREE

Ben dropped the face shield of his welding helmet before pointing the torch at the part in front of him. Sparks flew as flame touched metal, and he guided the tool with ease until the job was complete. Turning off the welder, he pulled his helmet off, feeling sweat bead on his forehead.

"Nice work, Weston." The foreman, Sonny Hartcourt, slapped a large palm against Ben's back. "That's all the welding we need right now. Think you can help Hanson over there with the rewiring?"

Ben nodded. "Sure thing. Can I take a couple of minutes to step outside and cool off first?"

Sonny smoothed a hand over his thin beard and nodded. "Yeah, okay. Go ahead and take your break. We're running ahead of schedule today anyway."

"Thanks."

Ben removed his welding mitts before heading toward the front of the office building. The other construction workers eyed him as he passed, but he kept his gaze set straight ahead, giving the impression he was oblivious to their curiosity. He stepped through the front and paused on the sidewalk, leaning his frame against a column. The air chilled his skin, and he welcomed the coolness of the day. The remodeling work generated a hot, musty environment inside, so the winter weather was a nice reprieve.

He hadn't worked a construction job in a while, but his skills came back to him quickly enough to reassure the foreman that he was qualified to do the job. After spending the last several years managing a successful business, the physical labor felt right, like slipping into a lover's embrace. Though he had the foreman on his side, he had to earn the respect of the other workers, but he was sure that would come. The job itself was the *in* he needed. Now he just had to figure out his next move.

Mr. Hartcourt helped him out by assigning him to electrician Mark Hanson. From what little Ben had seen, Hanson seemed quiet, his grumpy attitude ensuring that people left him alone. He had zero interest in making friends and only a little interest in his work, which meant he ran behind schedule often.

Ben hadn't been hired to the construction crew as an electrician, but he was more than qualified for the job. From what rumblings Ben heard among the crew, Mr. Hartcourt had another high-paying remodeling job lined up after this one. That meant the foreman was anxious to keep his crew on task and ahead of schedule when possible, so he needed someone to help speed Hanson along. Ben welcomed the opportunity to find out more about the man who was the target of his investigation.

Ben's phone vibrated in his pocket, and he pulled it out to see an incoming text from Luke.

Call me.

Despite being curious, Ben didn't feel the need to call his brother right away. They weren't allowed to take calls on the job unless they were emergencies, and Luke wouldn't want him to risk his cover by breaking the rules. He would wait until he was back at the motel before he checked in to see what Luke had discovered.

With his computer know-how, Luke often managed tech support and research for the Legends when they worked a case. Though Ben was boots on the ground looking into the case, Luke was doing what he could online to help out.

Ben pocketed his phone and turned on his heel to discover he was face-to-face with Mark Hanson.

"What the hell are you doing?"

Ben wasn't worried by his target's question or the heat behind the words. From what he observed in a short time, Ben knew Hanson copped an attitude with everything, even with Hartcourt to an extent. The man knew just how far to push with their boss before he stepped over the line toward unemployment.

Ben scowled at the man and straightened to his full six feet and two inches. To Hanson's credit, he didn't back down even though Ben topped him by several inches.

"Hey, man. Did you need something?" Ben kept his tone light, though his face was stoic, revealing nothing of what he was thinking.

"Just because you have your nose up Hartcourt's ass doesn't mean you can show me up and get me fired. Step back. Got it, newbie?"

Ben crossed his arms over his chest. "There's no reason for you to feel threatened. You're the electrician, not me."

"You think the rest of us don't see what you're doing? You're showing us up to get on the boss' good side. Better watch your back, kiss-ass. We don't put up with that shit."

Ben shrugged, playing like he couldn't care less about Hanson's opinion when he really wanted to punch the man square in the jaw. "I don't want your job or anybody else's. I have my own. Doesn't mean I'm not going to do what the boss asks of me. If it bothers you so much, maybe you should give it a try. Then you wouldn't have to worry about losing your job to a newbie."

Hanson flexed his hands, and Ben wondered if he was about to be punched. But then Hanson whipped around and retreated inside. Ben rubbed the back of his neck, thinking he just blew his chance to get closer to his target.

Working beside Hanson would give Ben an opportunity to talk to him. He didn't expect to be buddies with the man, but he thought he could steer the conversation to Hanson's son. In his experience, men who loved their children had no problem talking about them if given an opening, even if those men were pricks to everyone else. If Hanson viewed him as a threat, he would shut Ben out no matter what.

Thinking Hanson had enough time to cool off, Ben went back inside and set to work without comment. Hanson glared at him, then ignored him. It didn't stop Ben from assisting. And Ben made sure he did just that — assist. He didn't try to take over but instead followed Hanson's lead.

The shift was nearing an end, and Ben was no closer to getting in Hanson's good graces than when he started.

"Hey, man." Ben positioned himself in Hanson's line of sight, getting another glare for his effort. "I meant it when I said I'm not after your job. You're good, so I think I could learn from you if you can handle me working at your side some more."

"Save it. I'm not here to make friends."

Ben forced a laugh, hoping it didn't sound as fake as it was. "I didn't ask you out for a beer, man. Just work. No big deal."

Hanson narrowed his eyes. "Stay out of my business. You're not fooling anybody."

Though it was several minutes shy of quitting time, Hanson started cleaning up his work area. Ben stared at him curiously, but Hanson offered no explanation. Without a word to anyone, Hanson nodded in Hartcourt's direction and walked off the site. Not long after, Ben heard a vehicle start, the sound drifting away as the vehicle drove off.

"He has to pick up his kid."

Ben turned to see Hartcourt standing there, following Ben's

stare where he fixed it on Hanson's retreating figure and kept it there long after the man was out of sight.

"What?" Ben acted like he had no idea Hanson was a father. He hadn't been on the work site or labored beside Hanson long enough to know that information, so he had to play dumb to protect his cover.

"Hanson's son is a fourth grader. He's in an after-school program, and Hanson has to leave by five to pick him up. He's the first one to leave every day, but he's also on the job site before anyone else to make up for it."

Ben stood with arms akimbo. "And why you don't push him about his job performance."

Hartcourt glanced down at his boots before meeting Ben's eyes. "Keep that to yourself, all right? Hanson and his son have had it rough, so yeah, I cut him some slack. I know he has a shitty attitude, but he does good work even if he is slow."

"He is good. He's just prickly as hell and more than a little paranoid. He has it in his head that I'm out for his job."

"You challenge him. He's not used to that, but he'll get over it. Just keep doing good work, mind your business, and he'll stop giving you a hard time."

Ben nodded. "Okay. I'll give him some time and space. No problem."

"Glad to have you on board, Weston. Finish up your work there and then knock off for the day."

Ben shook his head. "If you don't mind, I'll wait and finish it tomorrow when Hanson's here. I don't want to step on anybody's toes, and this was his project to lead."

Hartcourt studied him a moment before nodding. "Yeah, okay. Head on out then. I'll see you tomorrow."

Ben cleaned up his workstation, collected his tools, and headed for the beat-up pickup truck parked at the edge of the property. The frame creaked as he climbed into the cab. He turned the ignition a couple of times before the motor kicked to life. He pulled onto the road in the direction of the Skyline Motel, ready to wash away the workday.

After Reagan researched places for him to stay while he was in Ivy Springs, he wasn't surprised to learn the motel was the lone choice as far as overnight accommodations. The town was smaller than Fire Creek, and he hadn't heard of it until this case. He kept his expectations low because he would spend little time there while working the case. But the motel was clean and well-kept. The room wasn't spacious but large enough for his needs.

Reagan made the reservation under the guise of being Sonny Hartcourt's assistant. The pretense kept people from questioning his cover too much. The owner was the one who checked him in when he arrived, and while Ben couldn't recall his name, he found the man to be friendly without being too nosy. He'd noticed a few vehicles in the parking lot, evidence of other guests, but so far, the owner was the only person he'd seen at the motel. He didn't mind the quiet, but the solitude made him miss the noise and chaos of his family more than he expected.

He parked the truck next to his SUV. The newer, sleeker look of the Tahoe made the pickup seem every bit as old as the classic model was. He'd paid cash for the truck when he'd gotten to Ivy Springs because the beat-up work vehicle fit his cover story better than the Tahoe. He was free to use the SUV for surveillance without Hanson connecting the vehicle back to him. Ben didn't expect the pretense to hold up for long in a small town, but he also didn't expect to be in this town long enough for it to backfire.

He stepped inside his room, locking the door behind him, and emptied his pockets on the counter, which stretched along a wall underneath a big screen television. His long strides carried him into the bathroom. Starting the shower faucet to warm up the water, he spotted the pile of dirty towels lying in one corner of his bathroom and frowned. He'd forgotten to stop by the main office to request more towels.

To keep his privacy, he'd developed a habit of declining housekeeping services wherever he stayed, even though it meant making his own bed and asking for towels when he needed them. He didn't mind tidying up if it meant no one was in his room when he wasn't here, though it was inconvenient at times like now when he was tired and in need of a shower.

Pocketing the key to his room, Ben stepped back outside, goose bumps rising on his arms from the chill that came as the sun went down. Dusk had yet to fall when he started for the motel's office. Before he got very far, he noticed a maid's cart outside one of the rooms a few doors down from his. Saving himself a couple of minutes and several steps, he shifted direction to head toward the cart.

The housekeeper stepped from the room, her back to him. Since she wore all black, her short hair gleamed a brilliant blond in contrast, the layers curling to add a bounce to the style. As he drew closer, he noted her petite stature, making her willowy frame seem delicate. He quickened his pace when she started to push the cart farther down the sidewalk. His long strides easily caught up to her, and he lightly touched her shoulder to get her attention.

"Excuse me, miss. Could—"

The woman's scream pierced the air, the noise jarring his eardrums enough to make him wince. Ben was momentarily stunned, so he didn't anticipate the woman's next move.

Her arm jerked back, her sharp elbow connecting with his abdomen. Whirling around, she slammed her foot onto his arch, and the heel of her hand swung up to connect with his nose. Ben saw an explosion of stars behind his lids as pain made his eyes water. His hands belatedly flew up to protect his nose, and something warm soaked his palms. He pulled them away from his face to realize it was blood. The distraction cost him because the woman shoved her cart until it slammed into his stomach, sending another round of pain through his body.

Doubled over, he heard footsteps running away from him and a shout rise from behind him.

"Charlotte! What the hell…Oh, shit!"

Oh, shit is right, Ben thought as he shifted to one side to rest his frame against the exterior wall of the hotel. He gingerly raised his head until he looked up at the covering over the sidewalk. His fingers pinched the bridge of his nose to try and stave off the blood now pouring over his face.

"Charlotte, he's a guest. I think you broke his nose."

Ben tuned out the voices around him. He wanted to head back to his room and assess the damage, but he didn't trust himself to move away from the support of the wall just yet. He did agree with the voice's diagnosis that his nose was broken. It wasn't the first time he'd had it happen, so he recognized the signs.

A light touch at his elbow had him lowering his hands. He tilted his head slightly down to see a slender hand holding a hand towel out to him. He took it and shifted his gaze to the person at his side.

He was unprepared for the wide, smoky eyes peering up at him, the mesmerizing depths capturing his attention and staring straight into his soul. A fanciful thought that he was staring into the face of an angel crossed his mind until he remembered how this *angel* handled herself.

She didn't speak, and he realized how badly he wished she

would. Her eyes still resting on him warily, she stepped back gradually. He opened his mouth to stop her when the sound of sirens pierced the air, effectively breaking the strange spell she'd woven around him.

CHAPTER FOUR

harlotte watched in horror as the stranger gave the paramedic permission to reset the nose she'd broken. The wound had finally stopped bleeding, and she was surprised the man — who ended up being a guest of the motel and not an attacker — hadn't passed out from blood loss. Her stomach rolled to think she'd been the reason the man was seeking medical treatment at all. She wrapped her arms around her middle and silently prayed she didn't add to her embarrassment by vomiting.

"You okay?"

Wally watched her with concern, and she hesitated a moment before shaking her head.

"I'm so sorry. I have never done anything like that before."

Wally glanced at the stranger and smirked at her. "I have to say, I will worry about you a lot less knowing you can handle yourself against someone his size."

Charlotte frowned. "It's not funny."

Deep down, Charlotte was proud of how she stood up for herself, but her pride took a back seat to how badly she overreacted to a guest's request for extra towels. With her ear buds in, playing her favorite pop music, she hadn't heard him approach. When she felt the hand on her shoulder, her worst fear reared up, pushing her to fight for her life without waiting to assess the situation. Of course, if the man had been an attacker, her quick action probably saved her life or, at the very least, bought her a few precious minutes to find help.

The thought did little to assuage her guilt. She hated being afraid and hated even more that her gut reaction was to run away from anyone she didn't know regardless of the circumstances.

Wally patted her back. "Come on. Look at him. Anyone would be afraid if they were randomly approached by him, especially when it's getting dark."

Wally was right about one thing. The man was big. Compared to her five-foot-five stature, he towered over her like a giant. His skin was tanned, making his eyebrows and hair appear as black as night. His arms were muscled and strained against the seam of his sleeves. His thighs were like tree trunks, and his shoulders were broad enough that she wondered how he fit through the doorway of his room.

He was beyond intimidating. He was frightening. If he had decided to take his anger out on her, she would have been powerless to stop him. A shiver snaked down her spine, and she turned away as the crunch of his nose being shifted back into the socket reached her ears.

"I should pay whatever it costs to have the paramedics treat him. At the very least, I should have his clothes cleaned or replaced," she murmured so only Wally heard her.

"No need. If he pushes it, I'll comp a day or two off his stay, but he only has himself to blame. I told him to let *me* know if he needed anything. He's the one who decided to sneak up on you when you were alone."

"Ssh, Wally! He's going to hear you, and you're wrong. He had every reason to believe he could get what he needed from the motel's housekeeper. I'm the one who overreacted."

The paramedic's voice caught Charlotte's attention as she stepped away from the stranger. "You sure we can't give you a lift to the hospital? Just to check that everything's okay."

"No, but thanks. This isn't my first broken nose, so I know the drill. Appreciate you setting it so I didn't have to go to the ER. I just want to get cleaned up and turn in for the night."

God, his voice. Deep, warm, and sexy, the rich tones washed over her. He could probably read to her the most boring book ever written, and she would be held enthralled by the low timbre. The idea startled her enough to turn back and study him with a fresh perspective.

He looked scary, but he was also striking in the proverbial tall, dark, and handsome way. His dark hair was thick, short, but wavy. His eyes, equally dark, were intense and brooding, even while he was acting polite and friendly to the paramedic. Charlotte studied the other woman, talking to the man as a professional, but something about the paramedic's smile made Charlotte wonder. Was the man charming the woman with his southern charm? Didn't the paramedic see what Charlotte saw — a man who was equally attractive and dangerous?

Obviously not, since the paramedic continued to smile friendly at him as she spoke. "Okay. Well, if your symptoms get worse, don't try to be a tough guy and power through them. Get to a doctor to be safe."

He nodded, winced at the movement, and stopped. "I will. Promise."

Wally stepped closer to the paramedic and her partner. "Thanks, Tasha. Can I get you and Jeremy a coffee before you head out?"

Charlotte shouldn't have been surprised, but she was. Ivy Springs was a small town, but even she was amazed by how many people her boss knew on a first-name basis. Most of his time was spent at the motel or with Mona, so she had no idea when he found the opportunity to meet people, much less remember them by name.

Tasha looked over at Jeremy before nodding in Wally's direction. "Yeah, that sounds good. The temperature's dropping out there."

Wally led them over to the coffee pot, his voice carrying through the motel's lobby. "Charlotte makes the best coffee around, and there's always a fresh pot brewing. You guys are welcome to stop by anytime you're on shift."

With the others preoccupied, Charlotte focused on the stranger. Though he hid it well, she detected the pain etched in the lines of his face. He pinched the bridge of his nose and gingerly stood. Charlotte automatically took a step back, feeling vulnerable next to his considerable height and build. She forced herself to peer at his face.

"I'm very sorry."

He pierced her with a dark stare, the area around his eyes already darkening from his injury. But the dark irises seemed almost kind, as if he wanted to comfort her, though he was the one with the injury. "No need to apologize. I shouldn't have approached you like that. I can't be mad at you for defending yourself."

She almost wished he were a little mad. If anything, it would justify her fear of him. Then she might feel less guilty for breaking his nose. "I can pay to have your clothes cleaned or just replace them altogether if you'd rather not keep anything you bled on."

He chuckled, and Charlotte felt his mirth all the way to her toes. "They're just work clothes. As sweaty and dirty as they are, they probably need to be burned anyway."

She glanced down for a moment, her hair brushing against her cheeks. "I feel like I should do something. You know, to make up for stomping your foot and elbowing your stomach and well…for your nose."

He barked out a laugh and then grimaced. "Don't feel bad. My brothers and I have done worse to each other when we roughhoused.

If you want to make it up to me, you can tell me a good place to get some dinner, hopefully delivered to the motel."

Wally showed the paramedics out, and Charlotte watched them go just to have something to focus on other than the handsome man in front of her. "There are a couple of fast-food places with drive-thru windows a few miles from here, and then there's King's. It's a little hole-in-the-wall place which serves mostly pub food. They don't deliver, but you can probably get something to go."

"Then there's Mona's. I was about to head out there myself, and you both are invited."

Charlotte whirled around to gape at Wally. His invitation shocked her more than realizing she attacked a motel guest. Wasn't this the guy Wally wanted her to stay away from? Now, he was inviting the stranger to his girlfriend's home and putting her in a position to sit at the same table with the stranger she'd just injured. Before she refused the invitation, the stranger interjected.

"And what is Mona's?"

Wally puffed his chest, his mouth broadening into a wide smile. "Mona is my girl and a mighty fine cook. She's making her famous pork chops, and I guarantee they will make you forget all about your broken nose."

"Wally—" Charlotte began, but the man talked over her.

"I wouldn't want to intrude, and I'm not sure I'm in any shape to be good company. I haven't even had a chance to clean up from work."

Charlotte tried again. "And I—"

Wally shook his head. "Nonsense. It's the least we can do for you, being such a good sport about what happened. Besides, the more, the merrier where Mona is concerned. She always makes more than the two of us can eat anyway. I won't take no for an answer."

"Wally, I can't," Charlotte finally blurted, close to shouting just to get her boss' attention. "I have to finish up the last of the rooms, and then I'm sure Ms. Miller will have something for me to eat. I hate for it to go to waste."

Wally waved off her attempt to use her landlady as an excuse to refuse his invitation. "Just call Birdie and tell her to wrap it up for you to have tomorrow. You know she won't mind."

Charlotte opened her mouth again, but no words came out. Wally wasn't wrong. Birdie Miller would have food waiting for her, but Birdie always cooked enough for several people. Since moving into the woman's garage apartment, Charlotte had been treated to many home-cooked meals under the guise that the food would spoil because Birdie couldn't possibly eat it all. Birdie had gotten used to cooking for her husband and boys over the years, and now that she lived alone, she'd not learned to prepare smaller portions.

Charlotte's eyes pleaded with Wally to let her off the hook, but he chose to focus on the stranger to wait for a reply. She almost whimpered in frustration when the stranger addressed her.

"I'm game if you are."

Charlotte raised her gaze to meet his before she thought better of it. His expression had softened, his eyes lightening to a warm, molten chocolate meant to reassure her. He smiled, and she blinked at how potent the simple gesture was. *How could one man be so scary and so devastating at the same time?*

Once he had her attention, he continued. "If they don't mind holding dinner up for us, I can follow you to Mona's house after you finish your work and I clean up."

Charlotte opened her mouth to refuse, but Wally interrupted her this time. "Great. I'll call Mona and let her know. I'll even call Birdie for you, Charlotte, so you can get back to your work."

Wally hurried to his office to make the call, leaving her alone with the stranger — something he said he didn't want to happen. Charlotte's mind whirled with how quickly the situation spun out of her control. She blew out a frustrated breath at a loss as to what to do now.

"I'm sorry. I feel like we railroaded you into this dinner."

She glanced at him out of the corner of her eye. "It wasn't you. It was Wally. He can be very pushy when he sets his mind on something. He feels bad about what happened. We both do. He prides himself on the hospitality of the motel, and he feels it's his personal mission to make sure his guests have everything they need."

"The special treatment isn't necessary, but I won't turn down a home-cooked meal. I don't get many of those these days. I understand if you decide not to join us, but I hope you do."

"Surprised you'd say that after I broke your nose," Charlotte grumbled.

Ben chuckled. "I told you, this isn't the first broken nose I've had, and it probably won't be the last. I can't complain, especially since I'm getting a home-cooked meal and some great company out of the deal."

Realizing there was no point in arguing, she finally nodded. "I guess I'd better get to work then."

"Before you do, can I get those towels from you first?"

She turned back to the stranger and felt a million butterflies flutter in her stomach to find him so close. "Of course."

Charlotte led the way down the sidewalk to where she left her cart. She heard the man's footsteps behind her at first, but then he was at her side, walking to the side of the walkway to give her plenty of space. She tried to relax the tenseness in her shoulders. It was hard to pretend she wasn't bothered when she felt his presence intently.

When they reached her cart, she managed to keep it between her and him as she gathered a stack of towels and passed them over.

"Thank you, um… Did I hear Wally call you Charlotte?"

She nodded but didn't offer anything more.

"It's nice to meet you. Do you mind if I call you Charlotte? You can call me Ben."

His hands brushed hers as he took the towels, and she shivered at his warm touch. Certain he was aware of her reaction to him, she felt a flush stain her cheeks. She quickly dropped her arms to her sides.

"Of course. It's nice to meet you. Let me or Wally know if you need anything else."

Her tension eased when he started back to his room, but then he paused. Her heart thundered in her chest when he turned back in her direction.

"I realize I'm a stranger, and you have no reason to trust me. But my sisters-in-law would kick my ass if I didn't tell you this. I'm probably going to be here for a few days, and I don't want you to feel like you have to be afraid of me. I would never hurt you. In fact, if you felt threatened or afraid, and I can help you in any way, please feel free to ask. I don't have to know the details. I just know you shouldn't have to be afraid while you're at work."

Charlotte felt a jolt as if someone shocked her with an electrical current. *How did he know? Did Wally say something to him?* She shook off the thought as soon as it crossed her mind. Wally wouldn't betray her confidence. The stranger was just guessing. But why would he offer to help if he didn't know?

He took his leave before she said a word or asked a question. Charlotte wasn't sure how long she stood there gawking after him, but some time had passed before she pushed herself to get back to work.

CHAPTER FIVE

"I spent almost a thousand dollars on flowers before she would agree to go out with me."

"Why would I agree when I was making money off you? A woman's gotta pay her bills."

Ben chuckled as he listened to Nolan Wallace and Mona Hillyard go back and forth in describing how they met and what led to their first date. The two were an odd pair, from the way they looked to the way they acted.

Wally was average height with thinning hair and a full mustache. He was jovial but direct, a what-you-see-is-what-you-get type of person. Mona stood slightly taller than her boyfriend, with her light brown hair and lovely face showing little signs of age. She was poised and well-spoken with a hint of mischief in her eyes and voice. She gave the impression that she knew more than the average person but was too classy to point it out to anyone.

Since stepping into Mona's home — a very neat one-story cottage-style house with antique furniture and flowers in every conceivable spot — Ben felt the couple's vibrancy. The two were obviously in love, and though they teased each other mercilessly, they also never missed an opportunity to show they cared. A kiss on the cheek, a hand to a back, a caress on an arm…all signs of a relationship which went deeper than companionship.

"What did you do with all the flowers?" Ben asked, enjoying the tale of romance where Wally met his match in the savvy florist.

"I got most of them," Charlotte interjected quietly.

Ben swung his gaze to the woman sitting across from him, as he'd done almost constantly since they sat down to eat the feast Mona prepared. Passing dishes of fresh salad, perfectly seasoned pork chops, creamy mashed potatoes, green beans, and homemade rolls, he'd had many chances to look into Charlotte's lovely eyes and brush his hands against hers. She seemed to withdraw from him each time, either because she felt the same pull he did or because she was uncomfortable with his attention. He wasn't sure of the reason, but he didn't like it. She hadn't spoken much since they arrived, so the sound of her soft voice now was refreshing.

"Every woman in town got them," Wally embellished. "The receptionist at the doctor's office, the ladies at the senior center, and even some of the guests at the motel. God knows, I didn't want them. They just gave me an excuse to talk to Mona. I would have spent every dime I had if it meant seeing her every day."

Mona smiled at him lovingly, her blue eyes sparkling. "You gave the flowers to everybody but me. Did it ever occur to you that I might have said yes to a date if I'd gotten some flowers?"

Wally looked horrified at the suggestion. "I couldn't give you your own flowers. That'd be like giving Charlotte a vacuum cleaner for her birthday. It's a terrible gift."

"You're saying my flowers are terrible?"

Wally glared at Mona, but Ben saw the corner of his mouth twitch as if he was fighting a smile. "I'm saying you can have flowers whenever you want. I wanted anything I gave you to be special, so maybe you'd thank me in that special way you do."

Mona rolled her eyes, and Ben laughed. He noted Charlotte's blush at Wally's innuendo, and Ben became fascinated with the way the light pink rose up her neck and infused her cheeks.

"On that note, I think it's time for coffee and dessert. Who wants some of my homemade apple pie? It's Wally's favorite."

"Add ice cream to mine, okay, babe?" Wally requested.

"Of course," Mona said with a smile meant only for him. "Ben, what about you?"

He nodded in Mona's direction. "Apple pie sounds great, and I wouldn't mind ice cream on mine either as long as it's vanilla."

Mona scoffed. "As if I would put any other kind on my apple pie. What about you, Charlotte?"

Charlotte leaned back in her seat, a delicate hand placed over her trim abdomen. "I couldn't eat another bite, so I'll pass this time. Thanks, though."

"I'll wrap up a piece for you to take home for later."

Charlotte shook her head. "No need. Ms. Miller will have something sweet waiting for me when I get home. Just save the apple pie for Wally."

"Wally doesn't need any more meat on his bones the way you do, sweetheart. If you don't eat it when you get home, you can warm it up tomorrow."

Charlotte dropped her protest as Mona left the dining room. Ben imagined she knew first-hand what he'd guessed — that no one won an argument with the sassy Mona.

"I heard you mention Ms. Miller before. Who is she, exactly?"

Ben was pleased he achieved what he hoped for with his question. Charlotte turned her eyes toward him. They were wide set in her face, the depths changing each time he looked at them. Sometimes they were a bright, almost icy blue. Other times they were a deep smoldering gray. And then times like now, they were an intriguing combination of the two, reminding him a bit of Ziggy's soft fur. He had yet to figure out how the changing colors aligned with Charlotte's temperament, and he wondered if he'd have time to figure it out before he closed his case and went home.

"Birdie Miller is a widow who has lived in town since it was founded, I think," Wally answered for Charlotte. "She's a sweet lady, but she lives on a fixed income. She told Mona she wanted to rent a garage apartment she had on her property, but she was nervous about who might rent it. So Mona and I help her find tenants when she needs them. Charlotte has been a perfect fit for her."

Mona returned with the dessert, but Ben was too busy watching Charlotte to start eating. Her blush deepened under Wally's simple praise, and she shifted in her seat slightly, a sign she was uncomfortable with the conversation. Mona picked up the dialogue as if she'd been in the room the entire time instead of in the kitchen preparing dessert.

"Birdie has outlived her whole family, so several people in town look out for her. Charlotte helps her with the upkeep of her house and the lawn work. She gives Birdie someone to cook for. Birdie is a fantastic cook. Her chicken cordon bleu will make you want to slap your momma, it's so good."

Ben chuckled. "Is it better than your pork chops? Because those were some of the best I've ever had."

"Thank you, and no. Her chicken is great, but my pork chops are exceptional. So is my pie so eat up."

He felt a little strange eating in front of Charlotte while she sat quietly watching, but one bite of the warm pie and the cool vanilla bean ice cream made the poor etiquette tolerable.

"How long are you planning to stay in Ivy Springs, Ben?" Mona asked after a few moments of comfortable silence.

"At least until the job is done."

Ben easily slipped into his cover story, a mixture of truth and fiction that he could hold to regardless of who he spoke with. His ability to slip into any persona he needed to be at any time made him better than his brothers at undercover assignments.

"I took a job with Sonny Hartcourt Construction," he continued. "We're working on a remodel of an office building on Grand Boulevard. I was looking for a change, so my previous boss recommended Mr. Hartcourt. I'm working for him under a trial basis. If it all goes well, I'll stick around."

"Where's home for you?" Wally asked.

"Alabama. I have some family near Montgomery." The half-truths slid from his lips convincingly, but he watched the expressions on his hosts' face for any signs of suspicion. He didn't mind them asking questions to get to know him, but if they suspected he wasn't who he claimed to be, he would have a problem on his hands.

"Tell us about your family, if you don't mind," Mona asked. "It's not every day we get newcomers to town."

Ben was prepared for basic questions about who he was. If Mona, Wally, or even Charlotte delved too deep into his personal life, he might have a problem keeping his story straight.

"There's my dad. He's the one near Montgomery. I have three older brothers. They're all married and live all over. Two of them have a son each. My mom died when I was young, so it's just been my dad, my brothers, and me for as long as I can remember."

Ben felt Charlotte's eyes on him, and he resisted the urge to meet her gaze. She had avoided looking at him as much as possible all evening. He felt her eyes on him whenever she thought he wouldn't notice, and he figured if he caught her stare, he'd spook her. He sensed she didn't trust easily, and though he wasn't sure why, he wanted to earn her trust.

"Have you worked in construction long?" Wally asked.

Ben chewed his last bite of pie and pushed the plate away from him. "No. I started working in retail. I sort of fell into construction work, and I like the physical labor. It feels good to use my hands and see the finished result."

Wally raised an inquisitive brow. "How do you like working for Hartcourt? I've known his family a long time."

Ben had picked up on a note of derision in Wally's tone. "I take it you don't think too highly of his family."

"I don't. His old man is some kind of financial advisor. A slick son-of-a-bitch. Some friends of mine invested their retirement funds with him, and he lost it all. Sonny's mom is a timid little thing. Rumor is she married old man Hartcourt for his money. They only had two kids, Sonny, and a daughter, Rhonda, I think her name is. She up and left town. I think she's married, but she doesn't come back as far as I know. I think Sonny does well for himself, but I know his old man was disappointed Sonny didn't follow in his footsteps."

"I don't know about any of that," Ben returned truthfully. "Mr. Hartcourt seems all right. Seems to care about his employees. There's one guy whom he lets work an adjusted schedule so he can be there for his kid."

"What are you going to tell him when he asks about your face tomorrow?"

Wally grinned, and Ben chuckled. "I'll tell him the truth. I acted stupidly and got a broken nose for my trouble."

Charlotte buried her face in her hands and groaned dramatically. Then she looked pleadingly at Mona. "On that note, I'll think I'll help you clean up and be on my way. I want to check in on Ms. Miller before I turn in for the night."

"I'll help too," Ben offered. "It's the least I can do to thank you for the delicious meal and the hospitality."

Charlotte pinned him with a stare meant to tell him something — too bad he didn't know her well enough to figure out what that something was.

She was quick to enlighten him. "It's not necessary. There's not many. I can take care of them."

Mona stood. "There's no way I'm going to turn down free help with the dishes. I love to cook, but I hate the clean-up. Ben, thank you for agreeing to help Charlotte out. Two pairs of hands can get the job done faster. Come on, Wally. Let's go find a movie to watch while we wait for these two."

Ben detected a matchmaker in their midst as Mona winked in his direction before she pulled Wally from the room. He began collecting the dishes from the table before Charlotte protested further. Taking them to the kitchen, he lightly scraped the bits of food sticking to the plates into the garbage can. Charlotte came into the room and looked anywhere but at him. She pointed to the dishwasher behind him.

"She has a dishwasher, but a couple of her serving pieces aren't dishwasher safe. The plates and utensils should be though."

He twisted to glance at her over his shoulder and was rewarded with a view of her rounded ass filling out her black slacks. She had a petite frame, but certain parts of her body were nice and curvy, like her ass and her tits. Both would be nice handfuls for him, and Ben felt his cock twitch behind the zipper of his jeans.

He cleared the sudden clog in his throat. "If you'll just set them by the sink, I don't mind washing while you dry and put away. You probably have a better idea of where things go than I do."

"I have a general idea," she admitted. "Wally and Mona have me over a lot. I think they feel sorry for me."

"I don't believe it for a second. I've spent the evening watching you with them. You act more like family."

He was rewarded with a partial smile tweaking the corner of her pink lips.

"I think I'm starting to feel like they're family. They've been good to me."

Ben filled the sink with sudsy water, watching Charlotte out of the corner of his eye. "How long have you known them?"

He pretended not to notice her hesitation.

"I came to town over a year ago. I noticed an ad where Wally needed someone to clean rooms. I applied, and he took a chance on me. Then he helped me find the apartment at Ms. Miller's. And the rest is history."

"What made you decide to settle down in Ivy Springs?"

For a moment, Ben thought she stiffened next to him, but when he glanced at her, she appeared as relaxed as she had been all evening. But something was off. He couldn't put his finger on what it was, and he surprised himself at how much he wanted to figure it out.

"I needed a change, and it reminds me of the town I grew up in."

An answer that wasn't really an answer. He was all too familiar with the tactic. Her explanation was vague while adding a personal touch to keep him from digging deeper. Anyone else would find her response sufficient, but he'd use the evasive move enough in undercover work to recognize it for what it was. Ben wondered what she was hiding and why she had needed a change.

"I like small towns too. The feeling that everyone knows everyone else. You're never alone. There's security in that," he said.

Her flinch was hard to miss. Ben hit a nerve with his off-hand comment. His guess was the words *alone* and *security* hit a little too close to home. Considering how she reacted to him earlier, he didn't think it was too much of a leap to guess she was worried for her safety.

The more they talked, the more curious about her he became. The idea of someone threatening or hurting her stirred his protective nature. His busted nose was proof she could handle herself, but that didn't stop him from wanting to help.

She wiped a dishtowel over the last platter and placed it in the cabinet just above her head. "Well, that's it. All finished. I've got to get going."

Watching her leave was the last thing he wanted. He had too many questions and a strong urge to get to know her better.

"I'll walk you out."

She shook her head, her blond waves bouncing around her face. "No need. Stay. Visit with Wally and Mona some more. They enjoy the company."

"I have to be going too. I have to be on the job bright and early in the morning."

She studied his face in silence, and he wondered if she questioned the validity of his words. He was a pro at hiding the truth from his expression. He didn't have to leave early, but he didn't want to stay without Charlotte. She wouldn't know that, though. All she would see on his face was sincerity.

She finally nodded and led the way to the living room, where Wally and Mona were cuddling on the sofa. The couple expressed their displeasure at their guests leaving for the evening. Ben and Charlotte had to promise to return for another meal next week before the couple bid them goodbye.

Once outside, Ben fell into step beside Charlotte, careful to keep a respectable distance between them. A car drove by, the headlights sweeping over them. Their strides carried them to her car first, and she paused beside it, her keys in her hand.

"I am sorry. About before. You've been so nice since it happened. I feel bad. I know you have to be hurting, but you don't act like it."

Ben tucked his hands in his pockets to keep from pushing her hair back from her face. The urge to touch the strands, to find out for himself how soft they were, was tough to control, and he didn't want to press his luck by making her uncomfortable with the move.

To distract himself, he tried to put her at ease about his injury. "When I was fifteen, I was playing football with my brothers. Two of them were on the varsity team at our high school, and they were trying to show our other brother and me some of the team's plays. I went running across the yard to catch a pass and misjudged the distance. The football slammed into my face, and I hit the ground. I had to have surgery to repair it. Compared to that, this is minor. I'll be fine, and you have nothing to feel bad about."

Her voice was light, warming him from the inside. "Sounds like your brothers are rough."

"Yep. Rough and tough, as our dad always said. They're older and pains in my ass, but I wouldn't take anything for them. They're the best. Just don't tell them I said so."

She chuckled. "You must miss them."

"I do sometimes, but we're accustomed to spending time apart. What about you? Do you see your family a lot?"

She sighed, the forlorn sound making him want to wrap her in his arms. "It's just me."

Her car beeped as she used her key fob to disengage the locks. "Goodnight, Ben."

He reached for the door handle before her and pulled it open. "Goodnight, Charlotte. Even with the broken nose, it's been nice meeting you."

He waited until she climbed inside before gently closing her door. Once she was driving down the road, he walked to his truck. He considered following her, but he managed to resist the impulse. Turning his Tahoe toward the Skyline Motel, he tried to push thoughts of Charlotte away. Though she was more pleasant to think of, he wouldn't be distracted from the case.

A little boy's welfare depended on him keeping his focus and doing his job to the best of his ability. Then when it was done, maybe he could turn his attention to the pretty blond housekeeper who was hiding a secret.

CHAPTER SIX

Charlotte's head bobbed along with the beat of the music streaming from her ear buds. Spritzing the blue cleaner on the lobby window, she swiped the liquid, dust, and fingerprints from the pane using a microfiber cloth. The sun shone high in the sky, dissipating the last remnants of dusk and promising a warmer day for the winter season.

The task complete, she exchanged the window cleaner for wood polish. Lifting a lamp from a side table, she dusted the dark finish until it shined.

The song reached its rock crescendo as she moved a vase of flowers from a coffee table and polished that surface as well. Placing the vase back in the center, she bumped the glass when she pulled back her hand.

"Oh, no!"

The vase tipped to its side, water and flowers spilling on the floor. She reached for the vase but was too late to stop its roll to the hardwood, the impact shattering the glass. A frustrated groan escaped her throat. Retrieving a garbage bag from her cart, she knelt beside the mess and started collecting the shards of glass.

"Ow!"

A sharp piece sliced her finger and lodged in the gash. She gingerly pulled the glass out and gaped as blood poured from the wound. She quickly reached for a rag and wound the absorbent cloth around her finger, trying to breathe through the pain of the injury. She jerked her earbuds from her ears and dropped them in her pocket. Tears welled in her eyes until she could no longer see the blood staining the cloth.

"Charlotte?"

Her head whipped up, and Ben's image swam in her sight before she wiped away the tears with her uninjured hand.

"What's wrong? I heard you shout."

He started toward her, and she panicked at the idea of him seeing her hurt and upset. Looking away, she pushed to her feet, struggling with one hand to brace herself. Ben was instantly at her side, his hands on her elbows to help her stand.

"I'm fine. It's no big deal. I'll put a bandage on it and get this mess cleaned up," she told him.

She tried to back away from him, but he held her firmly without hurting her. Ben lowered his head until they were eye-to-eye. With the way he studied her, she was sure he'd see the pain she was in. She dropped her eyes to focus on a button of his work shirt.

"You should go. I'll be fine, and I'm sure you have to get to work. I mean why else would you be up this early in the morning?" She sputtered a nervous laugh which sounded strangled to her ears.

"Work can wait. Can I have a look at your hand? I have experience in first aid."

She shook her head gently. "It's fine. I told you. I just need a bandage, and I'll be good to go."

She tried to step away again, but he wouldn't release his hold.

"Please. Let me have a look."

She hesitated, but the earnestness in his voice broke her resolve. She finally nodded. He grabbed a fresh towel from her cart before gently unwrapping the rag from her finger. The moment the pressure was released, the blood flowed freely, and Charlotte's head spun. Ben hastily wrapped the clean towel around her hand, cinching it tight enough that she whimpered. Spots appeared in front of her eyes, but before she said anything, Ben's strong arms encircled her waist.

"Just breathe, sweetheart. I'm going to lead you over here and let you sit down for a moment. Do you guys keep juice for the guests anywhere?"

"Fridge under the coffee pot," was all she managed as the world spun around her.

He lowered her to the couch, and she rested her head against the cushions. Her eyelids slid shut as she lifted a silent prayer that she wouldn't faint in front of Ben. His boots cast heavy footfalls on the hardwood as he moved around. She knew the moment he returned to her side, the heat from his body permeating her uniform.

"Here, sweetheart. Sip this."

He lifted a plastic bottle of orange juice to her mouth, his hand bracing the back of her head. The cool liquid slid down her throat, the acidic, sweet taste chasing away the dizziness. She took a couple of deep breaths.

"Thanks. I'm good now."

She gave him a small smile, but he still watched her with concern.

"You're going to need stitches."

Stitches meant a trip to the emergency room to see a doctor, which meant a sizable medical bill that she had no insurance to cover. She shook her head quickly but slowed the motion when she felt woozy again.

"No, please. I'll be fine. I'm sure it looks worse than it really is."

His brow furrowed, and she resisted the temptation to smooth it with her finger.

"Charlotte—"

She quickly interrupted him with a change in subject. "What are you doing here? Shouldn't you be heading to work?"

"What's going on?"

Charlotte had been so focused on Ben that she hadn't heard her boss come in the back door and through his office. Charlotte's tension eased. She could count on him to back up her decision not to go to a hospital. Wally hated doctors and refused to go to one. He loved to brag about how he hadn't visited a doctor's office since he was a child and broke his leg roughhousing with his friends.

"Hi, Wally. Sorry I don't have your coffee ready. I dropped a vase and cut myself trying to clean it up. Just give me a sec, and I'll get caught up on everything."

Her breezy tone earned her a stern stare from Ben. She ignored him, instead looking over his shoulder as Wally made his way over to them. Her boss' eyes widened when he spotted her towel-wrapped hand. The blood had seeped through, though not as much as it had the first rag she used. The pressure from the towel on her wound slowed the bleeding, and she would use that to validate her decision not to seek medical treatment.

"It's not just a cut," Wally said.

"She needs stitches," Ben told him.

She glared at Ben. "I told you I'm fine." Then she looked up at Wally. "It's nothing. The bleeding has almost stopped. I'll clean it with antiseptic, cover it with a bandage, and I'm good to get back to work."

"You should get checked out," Wally told her. "You were hurt at work, so I'll cover the bill."

"The bill? Is that why you're refusing to see a doctor?" Ben demanded.

Charlotte's eyes shifted back and forth from Wally to Ben. "It's none of your business! I said I'm fine. Let it go, okay? I have a mess to clean up and work to get back to."

The pain in her finger was hard to ignore, and the two men hovering over her made her feel smothered. This time when she pulled away from Ben, he let her go.

Wally shook his head at her. "Forget the mess. I'll clean it up, and I'll call Betsy in to cover your shift. Then you and I are going to the doctor."

"That's not—"

"I can take her," Ben volunteered.

"No." Charlotte blew out a frustrated breath. "You have a job to get to. So do I. Once I finish my work, I'll have my finger examined. Does that work for you?"

Wally addressed Ben as if she hadn't spoken. "It started pouring rain when I came in. You still have to work at the construction site?"

Ben nodded. "Most of the work now is inside, but I can show up late. Hartcourt will understand. I'll take her to get stitches, and you can stay here to take care of things."

"Will you listen to me? I'm not going to a doctor. Not right now," Charlotte insisted.

Wally ignored her protest and addressed Ben. "There's a twenty-four-hour clinic on the edge of town. You'll probably have less wait time there than if you take her to the emergency room. I'll call ahead and take care of the payment arrangements."

"You're not paying for anything because I'm not going anywhere," Charlotte shouted. "I'm not a child, so stop treating me like one."

Wally crossed his arms over his chest. "Fine. Then answer my question like a mature adult. How bad did you slice your finger?"

Charlotte stretched her mouth into a thin line. She wasn't certain, but considering the amount of blood soaking the towel and the pain she was feeling, she would have to admit the cut was severe.

Wally nodded as if she voiced her thoughts aloud. "That's what I thought. Stop arguing and go see a doctor. Say the word, and I'll take you myself."

Charlotte almost agreed, but common sense made her second-guess the decision. The motel couldn't afford to have the office unmanned during the day when people called for reservations and guests made requests. Closing the office for the time they were away at the clinic could cause issues for the business. She also didn't want Ben to skip work for her.

"I'll go, but I'm driving myself. I'll let you know what the doctor says. And I'm paying my own bill. I insist on it."

"I don't think you should drive," Ben interrupted, frowning at her. "You got lightheaded a moment ago. What if it happens again while you're behind the wheel?"

"It won't. I told you I'm—"

"Please don't say you're fine when we both know you aren't."

"He's right," Wally said. "Let him drive you. He can drop you off, and I'll pick you up when you're finished."

Charlotte sighed, seeing no use in continuing the argument when the men were this stubborn. "Fine. Let's get this over with."

She walked outside without waiting to see if Ben followed, though she knew he would. She stopped under the awning at the front of the motel and scowled at the pouring rain. The fat drops hitting the ground sounded like thunderous applause.

"Stay here."

Ben ran into the rain before she stopped him. With a moment to herself, she closed her eyes to the pain and gave herself a mental beating for not being more careful when picking up the broken glass. She knew better than to be reckless like that.

She stepped back when the Tahoe pulled under the awning and stopped in front of her. Ben opened the passenger door from inside, and she slid onto the seat before sending him a curious look. "What happened to your truck?"

"It's a work truck, and I figured you'd be more comfortable in the Tahoe. Buckle up and settle back. Do you know where the clinic is, or do I need to search for an address?"

She explained how to get to the clinic and then fixed her gaze to the scenery passing. She hoped he took the hint that she was in no mood to talk. In fact, the longer she sat in his SUV, the fouler her mood became.

It wasn't the pain so much. She had a high pain tolerance. The loss of her blood had made her woozy, but she'd recovered quickly. Yet, Wally and Ben treated her like she was too fragile to look after herself. It was a cut to her finger, for goodness sake!

The parking lot of the twenty-four-hour clinic only had a few cars, so Ben was able to park close to the door.

"Wait for me." Ben was out of the vehicle before she protested, but he was an idiot if he thought she was taking any more orders from him.

Using her left hand to release the door latch, she pushed it open with her shoulder, careful not to bump her hand. Swinging her legs out, she was ready to slide down to the ground when Ben crowded her space.

"Charlotte—"

She held up her left hand, palm facing out. "Don't. I'm not helpless. I cut my finger, sure, and I'll admit it's probably worse than I let on. But I'm not some fragile statue you have to handle with care. I can walk inside without any help. I've been taking care of myself long before I met you, so you can stop with the overprotective routine. You've dropped me off. Now you can go to work. I'm f—"

He lowered his head before she realized what was happening. His lips closed over hers, warm and firm. Her eyes widened in shock before the thrill of the kiss took over. She closed her eyes and relished the heat building within her. His hand cupped her cheek, his thumb smoothing her skin. Then he pulled away, leaving her fighting through a mind-numbing haze to figure out what just happened.

"What was that for?" Her tone was breathy, and her heart pounded in her chest.

"It was the only way I could think of to stop you from saying *I'm fine* again."

"Wh...What?"

"I'm not leaving you. I'll call my boss while we're waiting for the doctor to let him know we'll be late, but I'm not leaving you while you're hurt. I know you can take care of yourself, but it doesn't mean you have to. Come on. Let's get inside."

She had no argument left in her, so she allowed him to help her from the SUV. He urged her to go ahead of him toward the clinic, but she hesitated.

"So how bad is it really? I know I need stitches, but will it keep me from working? I can't afford that."

He pushed her hair behind her ear, his gaze softening. "It's a deep cut, and it'll probably limit you some. The doctor will be able to tell you more, so try not to worry until you get his instructions. It may not be as bad as I think."

She nodded, but she didn't believe him. He was trying to make her feel better, but she would rather have had a second kiss than a half-truth from him.

Oh, that kiss. For a moment, she'd forgotten she was in pain. She'd forgotten a lot of things, like where she was or why she was there. The kiss rocked her, and she had to admit her attraction to him was stronger than she thought. He was hot, but he was also kind and charming. His kiss, however brief it had been, was lethal, which made him dangerous to her peace of mind.

She should keep her distance, but it was hard not to be glad he'd stayed with her.

CHAPTER SEVEN

Ben drove his Tahoe where Charlotte instructed him before she fell asleep. He drove to the end of the driveway at the address she'd given him. Switching off the engine, he shifted in his seat to study his passenger. Her head rested against the headrest, facing him. Soft snores punctuated her breathing. Her bandaged hand rested in her lap while the other was trapped between her body and the seat.

Her blond hair fell in a curtain to shield her face. He gave into the temptation to lightly push the tendrils back over her shoulder, noting how silky the strands felt against his fingers. Her inky lashes brushed against her cheeks, creating an oddly fascinating contrast. Her lips were slightly parted and glistened as if her tongue had just swiped over them.

Something stirred within his chest, and he chalked it up to relief that she was no longer in pain. He hadn't joined her in the exam room out of respect for her privacy, but she'd given the doctor permission to update him on her care. The cut stretched along her joint deep enough to require two layers of stitches to seal the wound and restrict movement. The doctor had ordered something to manage her pain while they applied her stitches, but with the injury to her dominant hand, she would have a difficult time with everyday activities.

She had wanted to retrieve her car and drive herself home after the doctor released her, but Ben insisted on taking her home. He suspected she was still under the influence of the pain meds since she didn't offer much of a protest. Now that they were here, he loathed to wake her.

Through the windshield, he eyed the steps leading up to her garage apartment. They were wide and evenly spaced, so he could carry her. She would hate it, but he rather liked the idea. He would have to somehow get the key from her though, and he wasn't sure he could do that without waking her.

As he contemplated his next move, he noticed someone stepping from the house. With one more glance to ensure Charlotte was still asleep, he quietly opened the door and stepped out.

"Hello," he greeted.

The woman eyed him critically behind the large lenses of her glasses. If she measured over five feet tall, Ben would be surprised. She carried herself with a careful elegance like a woman who only moved when it was necessary. Her dark gray hair framed her round, wrinkled face, but her bright blue eyes were sharp as they regarded him.

"How is she?"

Ben glanced at Charlotte before eyeing the woman again. "You know what happened?"

"Wally called. I'm Birdie Miller. She rents the apartment from me."

"Nice to meet you, Ms. Miller. My name is Ben Weston. I met Charlotte at the—"

"Motel," Birdie finished for him. "Most men wouldn't help the woman who gave him two black eyes and a broken nose."

Ben smiled. "I'm not like most people."

"We'll see."

Ben wasn't sure what the hidden meaning was behind her words, but he decided not to concern himself with it. He walked around the front of his SUV and stopped, his hands settling on his hips.

"The cut was deep enough for her to need two layers of stitch-es. The inner layer will dissolve on its own. She has to keep the outer layer dry for the next forty-eight hours, and then she has care instructions to keep it clean and treated with ointment. The biggest concern is infection, so she'll have to be careful until she goes back to the doctor to have the outer layer of stitches removed. They gave her something for pain while she was at the clinic, but she can manage with over-the-counter meds from now on. She was pretty tired when it was all said and done and fell asleep on the way home."

Birdie nodded as if none of the information was a surprise. The woman watched him with an assessing stare, and Ben had an odd sensation that she knew everything about him, including the truth about his identity. There was no way she could know that, but Ben decided Birdie Miller was someone he had to be very careful around.

"I was about to help her get settled in her apartment," Ben added.

"Bring her in here for now. I'll watch over her while she rests, and then she can go to the apartment when she's ready."

Birdie turned and shuffled back inside the house, leaving the door wide open. Ben wasn't sure whether to laugh or run screaming from the odd woman, but since caring for Charlotte was his priority, the choice was taken out of his hands.

Charlotte stirred when he opened the passenger door. She turned groggy eyes to meet his, and he felt the power of those unusual eyes punch him in the gut.

He waited until the remnants of sleep fell away, and she sat up straighter, wincing when she moved her injured hand.

"Hey. You're home, but Ms. Miller wants you to come inside her house. I think she wants to be nearby, so she can help you with anything while you rest some more."

Charlotte grimaced. "I'm surrounded by a bunch of mother hens."

He grinned. "I don't know. It's kind of nice to know you have so many people who care about you."

She sighed. "It is. Don't get me wrong. I love them all. They've been very good to me since I moved here, but it does feel like my life is not my own sometimes."

Ben understood the sentiment all too well, but he kept that tidbit to himself. "I was going to carry you inside, but since you're awake, I'll give you the option of walking or being carried inside like a princess."

Her look of horror made him laugh. "I'm capable of walking, thank you."

He stepped back and held out a hand to help her step down from the Tahoe. She slipped her tiny palm in his but pulled back at the last minute.

"Before we go inside, I wanted to say something. I do appreciate your help today, but the kiss…"

Her voice trailed off, and he could imagine where the conversation was going. He wasn't going to make it easy for her, so he waited. She cleared her throat and started again.

"I get you did it to get me to stop arguing, but—"

"That's not why I kissed you. Well, not the only reason."

Her shocked expression gave him some satisfaction. He pegged Charlotte as someone who needed to be in control of her circumstances. Being with her all morning gave him a glimpse into what she was like when she let down her guard. She was more approachable and receptive.

"I don't understand. You said—"

"That I kissed you, so you'd stop talking. What I didn't say was that I've been wanting to kiss you since we had dinner with Wally and Mona. I figured it would be one hell of a kiss, and for me, it was."

The smoky irises of her eyes shifted from a steely gray to a deeper blue. Her breath hitched, and the pulse in her throat quickened. Hunger pooled in his belly, and he was sure the responding smile curling his lips held a hint of the predatory feeling he was experiencing.

"Ben, I don't...I mean, it's not a good idea...It's..."

The way she stumbled over her words reminded Ben he was being unfair, laying his intentions out there the way he was after the day she'd had. He didn't regret telling her, even if it did throw her for a loop.

He liked Charlotte. A lot. He wasn't in Ivy Springs to start something with a woman, but after hearing her painful cry that morning and seeing her hold onto her inner strength despite her hurt, he couldn't stay away from her. He barely knew her, suspected she held many secrets she may never trust him with. But tasting her lips, seeing her smile, and feeling her eyes on him were enough. For now.

"I won't kiss you again."

Her head whipped up, her lips parting in a silent *oh*.

"You won't?"

He couldn't tell if she was relieved or disappointed, and he guessed she wasn't sure either. He leaned in until their breaths mingled in the air.

"I won't. Unless you ask me to. And Charlotte?"

"Yeah?"

The one word was breathless, and Ben had a sudden image of her in his arms, in his bed, lost in the throes of passion, struggling to catch her breath amid the delicious sensations she would feel when his hands and his lips explored every inch of her. His cock stirred behind his zipper, but he ignored it for now. His focus was all on her.

"Make no mistake, sweetheart. I want you to ask me to. Sooner rather than later."

Ben enjoyed watching the play of emotions across her face. He pulled back to give her some breathing room and reached out his hand.

"We'd better get inside before Ms. Miller comes looking for us."

Charlotte visibly swallowed. "She's been watching us. She can stand at her kitchen window and see everything on this side of the house."

Ben chuckled, not at all surprised at that bit of news. "I get the impression she doesn't like me, or at the very least doesn't trust me."

"She doesn't." Charlotte took his hand and slid down from the seat. "She doesn't trust anyone, and she starts out hating everyone until they prove they're worthy of being liked."

He stepped back a bit, and she followed. Once she was clear of the door, he pushed it closed and tucked her hand under his arm.

"She likes *you*, though, right?"

Charlotte nodded and chuckled. "Yes. It took a few months to win her over, but we're friends now. Sometimes she feels more like a mother than a friend, but — and don't tell her I said this — I don't mind. She's a tough nut to crack, but she's a good one to have in your corner."

"Any advice on winning her over?"

She glanced at him with a mischievous gleam in her eyes. "Nope. You're on your own."

"Well, considering how much she cares for you, she has to be someone special. I look forward to getting in her good graces."

"You're planning to be in town a while?"

He was sure she meant it as a joke. "You saying it'll take a while to befriend her?"

"It might. With Ms. Miller, you never know."

He returned her smile. "I'm planning to be in town for as long as it takes."

"As long as it takes for what?"

"As long as it takes to find what I'm looking for."

He squeezed the hand snaked around his arm and led her to the open door.

CHAPTER EIGHT

harlotte accepted the shopping bag from the clerk with a shy smile. Her purchases weren't heavy — deodorant, shampoo, a disposable razor, and more antibiotic ointment for her finger. All things she could have gotten at the box store along with her groceries and other essentials, but she liked shopping the mom-and-pop convenience store.

The same two clerks ran the cash register each time she came in. The store was never packed with customers. The prices were reasonable. And it gave her a sense of belonging, something she craved more and more with each day that passed.

Snuggling her coat closer to her body, she braced herself for the burst of cold assaulting her when the door opened. She stepped onto the sidewalk, marveling at how the temperature was frigid when the sun was so bright. Once the icy breeze died down, she found the walk along Main Street pleasant.

Many of the shops were closed on Sunday afternoon, but people milled about. She kept her head down, so no one would be tempted to speak with her. Not that she knew very many people. Even after living in Ivy Springs for a year, she led a solitary life, meeting and befriending only a select few. It was safer that way. Friends asked questions she wasn't prepared to answer. Others were content to gossip about her, but she'd never minded the gossip mill. There were times it came in handy.

The smell of baked goods and freshly brewed grounds drifted on the wind, her cue that she was close to the coffee shop and the spot where she parked her car. Drawing her keys from her coat pocket, she pointed the key fob in the direction of her car. Then she stumbled.

"Ben? What are you doing here?"

The man who occupied way too many of her thoughts lately leaned casually against the passenger door of her car. She hadn't seen him since she sliced her finger, and he looked better in person than the fantasy living in her head.

His legs were stretched in front of him, crossed at the ankles. He held a to-go cup from the coffee shop in one hand while the other was hidden in the pocket of his bomber jacket. His wavy hair was tousled by the wind, giving him a sexy, rumpled vibe which warmed her insides. He flashed a smile at her rude question, and Charlotte felt her insides turn mushy.

"I recognized your car when I came out of the coffee shop. I wasn't sure where you were or how long you'd be. But since I'm in no hurry, I thought I'd wait a few minutes on the chance that I would see you and say hello."

She stood wide-eyed, shocked that he would, first, notice her car, and second, wait specifically for her. Unsure what to say, she forced her feet forward, unlocked the car doors, and deposited her purchases in the back behind the driver's seat. Feeling him watching her expectantly, she finally met his gaze with a slight smile.

"Hi." She barely refrained from cringing at her lame greeting.

Since his broken nose had healed enough for the bruising to disappear, she noticed how his eyes were darker than any she'd ever seen. Brown wasn't an adequate description. They were blacker like a dark roast coffee, the depths intense but soft and tempting — an unsettling combination. He had twisted around to face her over the top of her car, and though the vehicle was between them, he was too close for her comfort.

"How's the finger?"

She lifted the bandaged appendage. "Better, but the doctor wants to wait until next week to take out the stitches. It's awkward having to work around it, but I've adjusted."

He studied her for the next several minutes, a soft half-smile curving his lips. A flush crept up her neck, though she wasn't sure why. The silence was awkward, at least for her, but his gaze wasn't leering or inappropriate. It was just...direct, and she was unsure what he expected from her.

"Walk with me."

Certain she'd misheard him, she blurted, "What?"

His smile widened. "Walk with me. Unless you're in a hurry or have somewhere else to be."

She frowned. "You get that it's kind of cold to be walking around, right?"

Ben chuckled. "We don't have to go far. I was on my way to Whimsy just down the sidewalk."

"The bookstore?"

This man kept surprising her. Or maybe she just kept putting him in a stereotypical box where he didn't belong. He struck her as someone who could lose himself in the action of a sporting event versus the pages of a book. Realizing he was a reader appealed to her. The more she learned about him, the more she liked.

She tilted her head to one side. "The bookstore isn't open on Sundays."

He sipped his coffee, looking very pleased with himself. "It is today. I passed by there on my way to the coffee shop, and the open sign was all lit up."

"Oh, um, I don't know. I just..."

Her mind searched for a plausible reason for not joining him, but an idea never materialized. The truth was she'd been wanting to visit the quaint store but was never able to get there during its business hours. To visit it with Ben at her side sounded perfect, even if it was a danger to her peace of mind.

"Come on. I was on my way there anyway, and I would appreciate the company."

His voice washed over her rich and tempting, like fine wine she craved. She spent many weekends on her own, so his offer touched a lonely part of her she'd come to accept but didn't want to have.

Maybe this once. "Yeah, okay, but I don't have a lot of time."

She didn't really have any other plans for the day, but by implying that she did, she gave herself an out if being with him got to be overwhelming.

"Great."

With a warm hand at her back, he carefully led her across the street to the sidewalk. Traffic wasn't heavy at this time of day or in this part of town, but she felt protected as if nothing would touch her with him at her side.

He started talking once they were on the sidewalk, leaving openings for her to remark if she wanted but carrying the conversation when she didn't. She was content to listen, knowing anything she contributed would probably be lame and awkward.

"I didn't realize there was a bookstore here until this week. I was scrolling on my phone one night, and an ad for Whimsy popped up. I drove by here, saw the open sign, and decided to grab a coffee and check it out. Maybe you can help me choose a new read."

"I don't have time to read a lot, so I may not be any help."

Ben shrugged. "Then we can just sit and talk."

Whimsy was empty when they stepped inside. Charlotte glanced around, marveling at the quaint interior with beautiful book displays and cozy seating areas. The air smelled of vanilla and cinnamon, and while the atmosphere felt relaxed and elegant, she sensed an element of fun brewing underneath the surface.

A bell over the door signaled their arrival, and a striking woman appeared from the back. Her shimmering black hair was piled in a messy bun on top of her head, appearing effortless. Her make-up was impeccable with the earth tones enhancing her caramel skin and wide blue eyes. She wore jeans and a simple top with name brand sneakers adorning her feet. Even casually dressed, the woman was poised and refined, like an accomplished actress walking the red carpet. Charlotte felt frumpy by comparison, but the woman smiled as if having them walk into her store was the most exciting moment of her day.

"Welcome! Anything I can help you with?"

Ben shook his head. "I think we're just going to browse."

"That's fine. We're running a sale on children's books right now if you have an interest. Just let me know if you have any questions. My name is Tabitha."

"I love your store," Charlotte said. "I didn't think you were open on Sundays, or I probably would have been by here sooner."

"We're not open every Sunday. I usually only open when my husband is working. I like to keep busy when he's on shift," Tabitha explained.

"What does your husband do?" Ben asked.

"He's a fireman. If I'm working, he and his buddies will stop by. Mainly to eat the treats my mom bakes for the store, but I like getting to see him."

Tabitha pointed to a display on the counter next to the register. Delicately wrapped items were arranged on a tiered stand, carefully labeled to show what they were. Charlotte noted the variety of treats including oatmeal bars, chocolate chip cookies, chess bars, brownies, and trail mix.

"Well, if your husband and the other firemen won't mind, I may have to try some of the treats before we leave," Ben said smoothly.

"They'll get over it, believe me," Tabitha said dryly just as a child's voice called for Mommy from somewhere at the back of the store.

"Excuse me. That's my daughter. I'll just check in on her while you browse."

"How does she know we won't shoplift something?" Charlotte murmured more to herself, but Ben was close enough to hear her.

He nudged Charlotte's arm to get her attention and then pointed to a dome light fixture in the corner where the ceiling met the wall. "Security cameras. She has them posted all over, and I'm guessing she can monitor everything going on from the back area."

"You noticed that?" She hadn't seen the dome until he showed her, and yet he'd already picked out every spot in the store being watched.

His lips turned up in a slight smile which sparkled in his eyes. "I notice a lot of things."

Charlotte swallowed nervously. "So, uh, is there anything in particular you're looking for?"

He seemed to carefully consider her question as his smile changed into a flirtatious grin. "Well, some time alone with you for starters. Anything else is just a bonus."

If any other man had pulled out a line like that, she would have rolled her eyes. Coming from Ben, the words were intimate, and butterflies dipped in her stomach. She turned away and spotted the children's section.

"Do you want to check out the children's books? You said you're an uncle, didn't you?"

"Yep, to two awesome nephews, but I don't have the first clue about picking out a book for them."

"I don't either, but between the two of us, we can figure it out."

"I'm up for the challenge if you are. Lead the way."

Charlotte was more aware of things that she'd never given consideration before. With Ben behind her, she was anxious about how she walked. Her steps seemed heavy, her posture slouchy, and her strides too short, requiring him to adjust his own to keep from bumping into her. Her oversized tunic over simple black leggings was meant for comfort and not style while he looked good enough to eat in his jeans and bomber jacker. Her face was make-up free, her hair unwashed and straight. He was clean shaven, his hair wind-blown enough to be sexy and not messy.

Her insecurity had her wondering why he wanted to spend time with her. He could choose someone prettier and more confident, but here he was standing next to her among the aisles of bookshelves.

She shoved her negative thoughts aside and focused on the task at hand. "How old are your nephews?"

"Jax is five, and Dylan is a little over a year old. Jax is full of energy all the time and talks non-stop. Dylan is more relaxed, more serious, but way more curious than a kid his age needs to be." Ben chuckled. "They're so different, but they're best friends, if you can believe it. I think Jax would clock anybody who tries to mess with his cousin."

Charlotte felt a pang of envy at how Ben spoke of his nephews with such affection. She barely remembered feeling that kind of love in her life.

"You seem close to your family." She scanned the book covers as she spoke, selecting one or two which caught her eye.

"I'd trust them with my life. We may not be the most conventional family, but it works for us."

She glanced at him over her shoulder. "Why do you say that?"

Instead of answering, he showed her his phone. The photo on

the screen was of Ben with three other men around his age and size and an older man sporting white hair and a fit frame. Even smiling, they were a formidable group. Handsome, but intimidating. And that's where the physical similarities between the men ended.

"My brothers and the man who essentially raised us. We took this on a bachelor trip before my brother Luke got married." He pointed to the man with the icy blue eyes as he said Luke's name.

"Since I don't see any type of physical resemblance whatsoever, I'm guessing you're adopted."

"Not exactly. We were raised as brothers, but we never made it legal. Anyway, the guy in the middle. His name is English Barlowe, but we call him Gish. He took us in and raised us in his small studio apartment above the bar he owned."

She raised a quizzical brow. "You lived above a bar? I see what you mean about unconventional."

"Oh, yeah. I can't imagine the State approving of someone keeping kids in a bar apartment now, but then, no one in our small town thought anything negative about it. Gish has this reputation for saving wayward boys in need of a home. Everyone calls us *the boys* even though we're grown-ass adults."

She chuckled. "Your Gish sounds like one of a kind."

The conversation lulled as they studied the selection of children's books. They didn't touch, but Charlotte's skin prickled from his proximity. She breathed in his scent every time he leaned in to see what book she selected. By the time they decided on a few, her stomach was twisted in knots, and her nerves sang with awareness.

He stacked their selections on his arm and tucked them to his side. "I have something for the kids. Now I need something for me. This way."

His free hand lightly grasped her elbow, and Charlotte felt a tingle shoot up her arm, causing her heart to quicken. His thumb lightly massaged a circle on her arm as he led her to the mystery section, and his touch was potent through the fabric of her shirt. He told her the type of novel he was looking for, oblivious to how his touch was messing with her equilibrium.

She wasn't sure how she managed to suggest one or two without sounding like a fool, but he listened as if the recommendations came from a book critic instead of someone who barely had time to read.

Once he decided what to buy, he glanced at her expectantly. "See anything you want?"

Charlotte shook her head. "I told you I don't read very much."

"Okay then. I think I have all I want for now. Why don't we sit and talk for a bit? I love the vibe in this place."

Ben set his stack of books on a table in a quiet seating area by a window. On either side of the table were high back chairs with dark blue upholstery and polished wood frames curving elegantly along the back, the arms, and the legs of the chairs. The window was framed with billowy curtains and offered a view of the lot at the back of the store. Charlotte expected to see nothing but an alley through the glass, but the space had been repurposed into a lovely garden with planters of various sizes having the type of greenery which survived cooler temperatures.

The space was cozy — and far too intimate for Charlotte's comfort.

"I really should be going." She started backing away, but Ben stopped her with a light touch to her arm.

"Can't you stay for a few more minutes? Please? Do you want a water or one of the desserts Tabitha showed us?"

She opened her mouth to insist she needed to go. But the earnestness on his face stopped her. She found herself agreeing to stay, and he walked over to the counter to pay for his books and to purchase them a snack. Tabitha was quick to appear from the back to help him, the musical sounds of a cartoon filtering from the back room.

Charlotte sat stoically as she watched Ben and Tabitha make small talk.

Why did this man leave her in such a confused mess? One minute, she wanted to keep her distance from him. The next, she felt drawn to him. The connection touched a part of her she kept closed off for reasons she could never share with him.

Allowing herself to become too attached to someone made her vulnerable. But the way Ben watched her, spoke to her, touched her…she felt safe. She felt exhilarated. She felt like she could forget the role she was supposed to play and step into one she always wanted to live.

Ben returned with a pleased expression as he placed their refreshments on the table between their chairs. He took the seat to her right, appearing more comfortable than she felt. He motioned for her to take a bite of her brownie while he sipped his water.

"You said you're not a reader. What do you do for fun or to relax?"

An answer was on the tip of her tongue, but she wouldn't voice it. It was part of the life she left behind, a life she couldn't share with him without risking everything.

"I don't have any hobbies. My life is kind of boring."

She focused on her hands where they rested on her lap, hoping he wouldn't sense her white lie.

"I don't think you could be boring if you tried."

A nervous laugh escaped her throat. "You barely know me. You're hardly in a position to know if I'm boring or not."

"I want to know you."

His admission brought her head up. "Why?"

"Damn if I know."

She smirked, her walls crumbling. She needed something about this man to be wrong, so she could find it easier to stay away from him.

"Tell me something first," she said. "Your brothers are all married. Two of them have kids. So why have you stayed unattached?"

"I could say it's because I haven't met the right woman yet."

Charlotte shook her head. "And you would be lying."

Ben chuckled. "True. Honestly, I don't know if I want to be married. I feel like there's a lot about my life that would probably have to change if I met someone, and I like my life. What about you? Why haven't you settled down?"

Charlotte sobered. "Because I can't burden someone else with the baggage I carry."

His expression revealed nothing, but she saw a muscle twitch in his jaw. He hadn't expected that kind of answer from her, and she was a little surprised by what she'd shared.

"You're good at that."

She blinked. "At what?"

He hesitated for a moment before he responded. "You have a knack for answering a question without really answering a question. Your answers never provide information. They just evoke more questions."

"It's how it has to be. I have to be careful about who I share things with, so I don't trust people easily. That's probably not what you wanted to hear, but it's how things are for me."

His expression hardened, and he regarded her thoughtfully. "I understand it better than you think. Remember what I told you about Gish? About his reputation for helping people?"

Charlotte tensed. She wasn't sure where he was leading the conversation, but she didn't like the change in his tone. "I remember."

"He taught my brothers and me to do the same."

She waited for him to continue, and when he didn't, she pursed her lips. "I never asked for your help."

"Nope, you didn't. But I'm offering it. Not just while I'm in Ivy Springs. But anytime, anywhere. If you find yourself in trouble that you can't climb out of, call me. I'll be there for you, Charlotte."

"Why?" The question seemed to leave her throat on a husky breath.

"Because if you're not in trouble anymore, then you and I can get to know each other better. And I really want that to happen."

CHAPTER NINE

Canned laughter rose from the television as the actors in the sitcom delivered lines that were lost on Ben. Though no guests were in the rooms on either side of him, he kept the volume at a decibel level that broke the quiet in his room without being disruptive or distracting. He'd stopped trying to watch the show hours ago, instead lying on the bed, with his legs crossed at the ankles and one folded arm on a pillow supporting his head. His gaze fixed on the ceiling, his thoughts whirling at a dizzying speed.

He should be sleeping. His workday would start soon, and his body felt fatigued. But his brain refused to rest. He relived his time with Charlotte, relishing the moments when she smiled, when she laughed, when she spoke in a soft, husky tone, or when her eyes shifted from smoky gray to the bright blue that he figured out appeared when she was happy.

Then he questioned other moments when he may have shared too much. Was it too soon to tell her he wanted to get to know her better and spend more time with her? Was it the wrong time to tell her she could count on him to help her out of whatever trouble she was in or with the secrets she kept?

He may have been insecure around girls as a teenager, but as an adult, Ben had never questioned himself when it came to women. He knew what persona to wear. He knew how to read them and know what they wanted, what they expected from him. He assumed the role they needed him to play until it was time to move on. Doubts were never a factor in his relationships.

Until Charlotte.

He knew very little about her, but something felt so familiar when he was with her. He once read a book that described two strangers who believed they knew each other in a former life because their connection was so strong. Ben didn't believe in reincarnation and all of that, but he believed some unknown force pulled him to Charlotte.

The universe might be telling him he was meant to be with her. Maybe the universe knew she needed his help, and Ben could admit he had a special place in his heart for "damsels in distress" as his family referred to them. But though he wanted to be there for Charlotte if she did indeed need help — and he would bet good money she did — he wanted more than that.

He wanted to date her, to have more opportunities to kiss her or hold her. He wanted to build memories with her. The strength of his desire for her surprised him. He hadn't expected to meet someone like her while he worked a case or at any other time in his life, for that matter. He was content not to have it in his life, and just because his brothers had found love, he had been convinced it wasn't in the cards for him.

Not that he was in love with Charlotte. No, that's not what his feelings were. But what left him confused and almost afraid was that he could see himself being in love with her. And depending on what secrets she was keeping, it might lead to disaster for him.

He glanced over at the digital clock on the nightstand, watching it until another minute ticked by on the display. Frustrated with his inability to rest, he pushed himself up and grabbed his laptop. Soon, he was lost in the details of his case, feeling a different type of frustration that he was no closer to having answers than when he arrived in Ivy Springs.

Using his finger on the touchscreen, he scrolled through the case research Luke had sent him. When his eyes grew tired, he scrubbed his hands over his face, his five o'clock shadow rough against his palms. After an hour of reading through the material he had committed to memory by now, his hand snaked around to rub the back of his neck.

The intel was routine, the same information they would find on anyone with a basic internet search and examination of public records. Mark Hanson grew up in Missouri and lived there most of his life. He married his high school sweetheart, but several years past and a few miscarriages happened before Caleb came into their lives. At the time, Hanson wasn't working in construction. By all accounts, he ran a successful investment company while his wife Delia hadn't worked outside the home.

After Caleb was born, the Hansons moved around quite a bit. They stuck to cities in Missouri until Delia committed suicide two years ago. Then Hanson and his son moved to Illinois, Oklahoma, Texas, and then Georgia. Ben attributed the man's restlessness to the grief he felt at losing his wife, and the boy's school records reflected it as well. Caleb went from being a model student to being quiet and withdrawn, his grades falling from excellent to fair or failing in some cases.

Luke had managed to get his hands on the investigation notes from Caleb's Child Protective Services file, but those didn't have much to reveal either. Ben didn't want to know how his brother managed to find the intel. He suspected Luke's methods skirted on the edge of legality, but right now, that didn't matter as much as finding answers.

According to the file, Caleb showed no visible signs of physical abuse. There were no records of broken bones, sprains, or even bruises outside of what a normal nine-year-old boy would have. Any signs of emotional distress were easily explained as a withdrawn boy missing his mother.

Interviews with school personnel and neighbors indicated Hanson had a temper, but no one had seen him taking his anger out on his son. The father and son were apparently inseparable. When Hanson wasn't at work and Caleb at school, they were always together. Caleb didn't take part in extracurricular activities, and his life was pretty much spent at home or at school.

His teachers indicated Caleb was sociable with the other students at school and even had one or two that could be classified as friends, but he never had much to do with any of them outside of school, which struck Ben as unusual but not alarming.

Ben opened a search browser on his computer and did his own internet search for Mark, Delia, and Caleb Hanson. He wasn't sure what he was looking for, and he was certain there was nothing new to find that Luke hadn't already dug up. But he looked anyway.

He lost track of how long he spent down the internet rabbit hole, but the time was wasted when it revealed nothing he didn't already know. He found an old photo of the small family that someone had posted on social media a year before Delia's suicide. None of the Hansons had social media, so the post hadn't tagged them or originated from profiles that might reveal new intel. But the use of their names in the post alerted on his internet search.

He stared at the picture for a while. Hanson appeared much younger than he looked now, and Ben was stunned to realize he seemed…happier in the photo. The idea of his grumpy, temperamental co-worker being happy was a hard notion to digest. Hanson had his arm around his wife, a woman of average height with reddish-brown hair and sparkling brown eyes. She had her arms draped over Caleb's shoulders, holding him close to her. The little boy's smile seemed genuine, but something about him nagged at Ben.

Since I don't see any type of resemblance whatsoever, I'm guessing you're adopted.

Charlotte's words flitted unbidden through his mind, and Ben sat up straighter. His eyes narrowed as he zoned in on specific details. Hair color, eye color, build, nose shape, eye slant, ear shape, smile, chin, hands…They told him everything and nothing, but it was enough for his theory to take shape.

He lifted his phone, dialed a number, and placed the call on speaker. He scrolled through his case intel while he waited for Luke to answer. When he came across the documentation of Caleb's birth, he paused, studying this image as intently as he had the family photo.

"Hang on."

Luke's gruff voice was almost drowned out by the background noise. Ben distinctly heard conversation and music and realized his brother must be working a shift at the Fire Bar and Grille.

Though their brothers Jackson and Easton ran the bar — Jackson being in charge of the kitchen and Easton being the favorite bartender — Ben and Luke helped out by acting as security on occasion. Most of the time, their presence was enough to keep the peace. Sometimes it took more than that, but because his brothers ran a tight ship, it wasn't very often they had to forcibly remove someone from the bar.

The background noise suddenly silenced, and Ben suspected his brother stepped into the back office.

"What's up?" Luke asked a moment later.

"When you were running background on Mark and Delia Hanson, did you see any red flags with their documentation?"

"Why are you asking?"

He wasn't surprised Luke answered his question with one of his own. His brother was reserved when sharing information until he fully understood a situation.

"The birth certificate and medical records you found look legit, but…"

Ben's voice trailed off as he wondered if he was grasping at straws in an otherwise deteriorating case.

"You think they're forged?"

Ben pushed the doubt away. "Yeah, I do. I keep thinking about something someone told me when I showed them a picture of us from your bachelor trip."

"Someone?"

"Shut up and listen. She said she figured we were adopted because there was no family resemblance with any of us, which makes sense. After all, we're not blood-related. I found a picture of Hanson with Caleb and his wife. They don't look like each other either."

"Really, Ben? You're basing this on a picture? That's weak, and you know it."

Ben threw out a frustrated breath. "Look, there's no evidence of abuse here, but I'm telling you, something is off about Hanson. So just follow me here. His wife had several miscarriages before Caleb came along. Then there's no record that they tried for more children. They moved around a lot, especially after the wife committed suicide. Hanson also changed careers from one as an executive to one as a manual laborer. The doctor who signed Caleb's birth certificate has passed away, so we can't question him, but according to my internet search, he was named in more than one legal case of malpractice."

"That's not unusual with obstetricians."

"But the cases weren't settled in court or out of court. They just went away. So what if...I don't know. What if he had the resources to make them disappear because people were paying him to forge birth certificates to hide illegal adoptions?"

"How does this relate to the case? What are you thinking?"

"What if the reason Caleb doesn't look like Hanson or his mom is because he looks like someone else? Another biological parent, maybe?"

Luke was silent. Ben set his laptop to the side and rose to pace the space beside the bed as he waited for his brother to arrive at the same conclusion that he did.

"One of them had an affair."

Ben stopped, a smile splitting his face. "My thought exactly."

"Okay. So let's follow this. Which one had the affair? The wife, and now that she's gone, Hanson resents raising the kid that's not his."

Ben folded his arms across his chest. "I don't think so. With the miscarriages Delia Hanson had? I have my doubts she could carry a pregnancy to term regardless of who the father was."

"So Hanson had an affair. Or maybe they used a surrogate," Luke added to the theory.

"A surrogate would make sense. Either way, let's say Delia is not Caleb's mother. So they moved around, so the people in their life wouldn't know that Delia didn't carry or give birth to Caleb. They had a birth certificate forged to support the lie. And the OB who signed the birth certificate is the one who put them in touch with the surrogate. Now that Delia is gone, Hanson resents taking care of a kid who isn't his. Or maybe the surrogate heard about Delia's suicide and is trying to get custody of Caleb away from Hanson."

"That's a lot of what ifs."

Ben deflated and dropped back down on the mattress. "I know. Can you tell I've run out of leads?"

"You sure you're not wanting some or all of this to be true because you can't stand the guy?" Luke asked.

"It's a strong possibility," Ben admitted. "The guy is an ass. A big SOB, and any time I've seen him and Caleb together, I've gotten a bad feeling. Hanson never interacts with Caleb, but they're always together, like he's afraid to let Caleb out of his sight. The kid's not happy. The visit from CPS tells us that. Caleb's struggling in school. He has no friends, no extracurricular activities, nothing outside of his house and Hanson. Something is wrong there. I can't let this go until I find out what it is. I can't be another person who walks away from this kid when he needs help."

"I get it."

Ben scowled. "But you don't agree?"

"Do I agree that Hanson is an asshole? Yeah. Do I agree that Caleb deserves better? Yeah. Do I think your theory has merit? Not really, man. Sorry. I think you're reaching."

"So what would you do if you were me?"

Luke swore under his breath. "Run it down anyway. You won't let it go unless we do."

"Thanks, man. I owe you."

Luke guffawed. "Damn right, you do. And payback starts now. Who's the "she" that you showed our picture to?"

"Nope," Ben responded. "Not happening. Instead, why don't you tell me how everything's going?"

"It's all good. English has checked in at the hardware store every day you've been gone. He said your managers have everything under control. Reagan said your monster of a cat is fine. I think Jax is trying to talk her into bringing the thing home with them."

Ben chuckled. "I don't think Ziggy will like that. He's a homebody."

"Reagan said she thinks he misses you. But he's a cat, so who the hell really knows? How are you holding up?"

Ben's hand reached up to lightly touch his nose, which had outwardly healed but was still a bit sore. "Other than getting into a fight, I'm good."

"What the hell? I hope you kicked their ass," Luke exclaimed.

"Not exactly."

Ben explained what happened with Charlotte and how that led to a dinner invitation with her, Wally, and Mona. He found himself smiling as he relayed the story, realizing the evening had been one of the more enjoyable ones he'd had lately, topped only by the time they spent at Whimsy.

He was beginning to count any time spent with Charlotte as enjoyable and something worth repeating.

Luke whistled when Ben finished. "Damn. You met a girl. Let me guess. She's the one you showed the family picture to. Wait until I tell Mel about this."

"There's nothing to tell. I'm here working a case. It's not my fault that my path keeps crossing with this girl. It's a small town. But speaking of Charlotte, think you could check into her for me?"

Luke chuckled. "Don't tell me she's one of your damsels in distress?"

Ben stiffened. He hated when his brothers gave him a hard time about his soft spot for women in need. It wasn't his fault that "damsels in distress" found their way to Ben and trusted him with their stories of trouble. If he could be of assistance, he never hesitated to help.

He thought of the women in his life who had found themselves in difficult situations. First, there was their family friend, Becky Lathan, who was given what she needed for a fresh start by English. Then came Reagan and her mother, Melody and her sister, and then Bailee and her grandmother. He shuddered to think of what might have happened to any of them if English, Ben and his brothers hadn't stepped in to help when they did.

"Look, I don't know her story, but I think she's in trouble. The people around here are very protective of her, and she's evasive if you ask her anything personal about herself. Check her out and make sure nothing serious is going on? Like I said, our paths keep crossing, so I need to know what I've walked into, don't you think?"

"I think you have your hands full with the case you went there to work."

Ben scowled. "I'm just asking you to check. That's all."

"Fine. You said her name is Charlotte. What's her last name?"

Ben froze as he realized he didn't know. No one mentioned Charlotte's last name to him, and it never occurred to him to ask. "I don't know. I never found out. I just know her first name and that she works at the Skyline Motel in Ivy Springs. Oh, and she rents a garage apartment from a woman named Birdie Miller."

"You know her landlady's name but not hers? Something's wrong with this picture. Got a description of her?"

Ben easily conjured an image of Charlotte in his mind. "Blond, short hair. Petite. Cute. Big smile. Blue eyes, but they're not a typical blue. They have gray in them, so they change colors sometimes. Stronger than she looks."

"Let me guess. She's hot."

Ben instantly remembered her pert breasts and delectable ass. "Yeah, she's hot, but that's not why I'm asking for a favor."

"Right." Sarcasm dripped from the one word, and Ben knew there would be no convincing Luke that his request had nothing to do with any attraction he felt for Charlotte.

Which was Ben's cue to end the call. "Look, I need to go. I got to get some shut eye before my alarm goes off."

"Take care of yourself, brother. Don't work too hard, and try not to lose your shit over this girl. This case takes priority over a pretty face."

Ben frowned. "I know that. That's not what this is. I'll get to the bottom of this case, but if I can help out someone else in the process, I want to do that too."

Even as the protest passed his lips, he didn't believe it. He did want to help Charlotte if she needed it, but his concern wasn't just an innate do-gooder instinct. His desire to know more about her played a small part in his request.

"That hero complex of yours is going to get you hurt one of these days. Just make sure the rest of us are around if that happens. We've got your six, brother."

Ben appreciated Luke's concern for his well-being. "I know. Thanks, man. Talk to you tomorrow."

Ending the call, Ben forced himself to move his laptop to a table to charge. He brushed his teeth, used the facilities, and made sure his alarm was set. Switching off the lights, he climbed under the thin sheet and heavy duvet. Laying on his back, he folded one arm and rested his head on his hand as he stared at the ceiling.

When his eyes finally closed in sleep, he dreamed of a beautiful blond who looked like an angel and kissed like a vixen.

CHAPTER TEN

en slammed his hammer down on the framing nail, venting his frustration. The day had been a bust, and he still had a few hours to go before his shift ended. He worked alongside Hanson again, and the man was more disagreeable than usual. He snapped at Ben at every turn, and Hartcourt had to step in once when Hanson's verbal assault grew loud enough to be heard over the construction site.

Any attempt on Ben's part to smooth things over or find out what bug Hanson had up his ass proved futile. By twelve-thirty, Hanson had gone to see Hartcourt, and within minutes, he drove away from the construction site without saying a word to anyone else. Hartcourt just ordered Ben to continue with the work Hanson left unfinished without any sort of explanation as to why Hanson left.

Ben considered that something might be wrong with Caleb, but there was little he could do to check into it, just short of walking off the site and risking his cover. He wanted to call Luke for an update, but Hartcourt was strict about the use of cell phones when they weren't on break. Distractions led to accidents, so it was a rule he wouldn't break as much as he wanted to.

Ben was left with no one to take his frustration out on except for the nails on the business end of his hammer. After a bit, he realized he was less angry at Hanson's unreasonable treatment and more irritated at himself for losing his cool. He was conditioned not to rise to others' taunts or bullying, but today Hanson had pushed him too hard. That, along with Ben's fitful night of sleep, had been enough to rankle his temper.

When the time came to clock out, Ben waved off invitations from the others to grab a beer somewhere. With his curiosity burning, he drove to Hanson's home and found a spot on the street to park and watch his suspect's house without being noticed. Well, unless he sat on the street for too long. There was a risk that a concerned neighbor would call the cops and report him for suspicious activity. If that happened, he'd have some fast explaining to do.

He only observed for a couple of minutes before realizing no one was at the Hanson home. Hanson's car wasn't visible, no lights were on inside, and no one was visible through the windows. From what Ben knew of the man, this was enough of a break in the family's routine to make Ben suspicious.

After a moment, he started his truck and moved down the street, turning on the next block to drive up behind the Hanson home. If he drove slowly enough, he could see Hanson's backyard through the line of houses on this street. All was still and quiet, which gave him an idea.

Taking another turn, he drove the truck into the dirt parking lot of a small church tucked away in the quiet neighborhood. The brick sign announced the location as Guiding Light Church with services held on Sunday mornings, Sunday evenings, and Wednesday nights. The church remained quiet on the other days of the week, such as this one, so Ben parked behind the church out of sight of passersby.

He set out on foot, careful not to attract attention, until he was able to approach Hanson's house undetected. He peered in the windows but noted nothing that he hadn't seen before — a house in complete disarray. On a hunch, he pulled a glove from his pocket, slipped it on his hand, and tested the knob on the back door. He was shocked when it turned in his hand without resistance. The lack of security could be the byproduct of living in the small town, but knowing how private Hanson was, the notion didn't seem likely.

Taking a deep breath, he stepped inside and quickly closed the door behind him. Careful not to leave evidence of his presence, he moved through the home, not sure what he was looking for but searching all the same. He took a few deep breaths to clear his mind and push away the frustration of his day to focus.

Other than clutter, dust, and a faint odor he couldn't name, he found nothing of consequence as he moved from room to room. He cleared the kitchen and living room. There was another door that was locked, and he decided not to break his way inside. He had the skills to easily pick the lock if he wanted, but he had no idea how much time he had before Hanson and Caleb returned home. For now, he would stick with what was in plain sight.

He moved to the bedrooms, looking through Hanson's first before walking through Caleb's. He searched the pantry closet before stepping into the hallway bathroom. Nothing appeared out of the ordinary, and he was ready to exit when his gaze fell on a box in the garbage can. His brow furrowed as he reached for the box of hair dye. The smiling face on the outside had dark hair that was more of the shade of Caleb's than his father's. Placing the box back in the garbage, he searched through the cabinet under the sink and found two unopened boxes of the same hair dye.

Removing his phone from his jeans, he took a picture of the box. He wasn't sure what his find meant, but he didn't want to leave without documenting it. An idea struck him. He tore off pieces of toilet paper and used one to place strands of hair from a brush lying on the bathroom sink. Returning to the master bathroom, he did a different piece of the toilet paper to do the same thing to the hair in the brush he found there.

Deciding he'd spent enough time searching the house, he made his way through to the back door.

He heard a car door slam, and he rerouted his steps to a window that looked out at the front. An SUV parked in the Hanson driveway, the back hatch open. Only a moment passed before a hand reached to close the trunk door, revealing a woman standing with Caleb Hanson at the back. She spoke to the boy as he shrugged his backpack on, but Ben couldn't hear what she said. Caleb nodded and started walking, his steps taking him around the back of the house.

Ben ducked out of sight into the pantry just as Caleb came through the unlocked back door. Since he left the pantry door slightly cracked, he watched the young boy drop his backpack on the kitchen counter, stop at the refrigerator to grab a soda, then wander to a different part of the house.

Once Ben heard the distinct sound of a video game, he stepped out of the pantry and through the back door, locking the knob before he pulled it closed. The door had been unlocked for Caleb to come inside when he was dropped off, but Ben couldn't leave it unsecured with the young boy there alone.

Careful not to draw suspicion, he jogged back to his truck, his mind whirling. His gut churned like he'd just discovered something critical to his case, but he wasn't sure what that was. Rather than driving back to the motel, he placed a call.

"Hey," Luke answered at once. "Good timing. I'm here with Easton and Jackson."

Ben didn't know where *here* was, but it didn't matter. His brothers were the exact sounding board he needed.

"Good. I need some perspective on what I just found. So Hanson left his shift after lunch today. His attitude was shit, which is saying a lot since he's never friendly. The thing is, whenever he's not at work, he's with Caleb. As soon as I could, I headed over to his place to do some snooping. No one was home. The back door was unlocked."

"So you went inside," Jackson finished for him.

"Right, just for a cursory look. The place is a dump, but there wasn't anything that stood out until I went into the bathroom, which is obviously the one Caleb uses. I found an empty box of hair dye in the trash and two more boxes in the cabinet. The color matches Caleb's hair more than Hanson's."

"Weird," Easton said. "But what does it mean?"

"I'm not sure," Ben admitted. "I mean, what reason would he have to change Caleb's appearance, but not his own?"

"Well, why does anyone change their appearance at all?" Jackson asked. "If they're on the run. If they're hiding."

"If they're bored with their look," Easton interjected. "I mean, women color their hair all the time. It's weird for a kid to do it, but maybe he wanted something cool like a friend of his has. It wouldn't be that big of a stretch."

"He's a fourth grader. I doubt he's worried about his hair. He's more preoccupied with video games," Ben said. "Anyway, I'm guessing Luke filled you in on my theory?"

"Yeah," Jackson responded. "You think the kid is not Hanson's biological son."

"Well, either that or Hanson is his dad, but his mom was never his mom. So while I was inside, I got some hair from their brushes. Think we can find a lab to do some DNA testing? I know it's a long shot, but it's all I've got at the moment."

"If it closes this case sooner, then we'll make it happen. I'll call Alex. They have a private lab they use, and he can get a rush on it."

Jackson's Army buddy, Alex Crandell, owned the successful Atlas Security. Because he and a few of his security operatives were aware of the Legends, Alex often helped Jackson and his brothers with cases.

"Thanks, brother," Ben said. "I'm not sure where to go from here if this lead doesn't pan out."

"Something tells me we're heading in the right direction even if your theory is not right," Luke interjected. "I checked into the mom like you asked. Nothing stood out except for one thing I thought was odd. The doctor of record for Delia Hanson when she gave birth and had her miscarriages is the same doctor who signed her death certificate."

"Did she die in childbirth?" Jackson questioned.

"No. She committed suicide," Luke said.

"Did you check out the doctor?" Easton spoke up while Ben processed the new intel.

"He died some time ago. He has family living in California," Luke answered.

"So why do we care if he signed her death certificate?" Easton asked.

"Because he was already retired when she died," Jackson returned.

Ben stayed silent. His mind worked through the different pieces, tossing them around in his head, looking for how they fit together. His brothers continued to talk, obviously not realizing that he didn't chime in. Their back-and-forth was a piece of home that he'd been missing since beginning this case. The banter was welcomed background noise, familiar in its chaos, allowing him to think.

"Ben. Ben. You still there?"

Ben turned his attention back to the phone call. "Yeah, sorry. Just thinking."

Jackson continued. "I texted Alex. He has someone in the area where you are. He'll meet you at the motel in a couple of hours to get the samples."

"Great. Thanks, man. Listen, I'll talk to you guys later."

"Hold up, Ben," Luke said.

With the shift in background noise, Ben guessed his brother took the call off speaker phone.

"Listen, I checked into your girl."

"She's not my girl," Ben grumbled.

"Keep telling yourself that, brother. Anyway, Charlotte Redding came up clean. At least for the last year or so. Beyond that..."

Luke's voice trailed off, and Ben sat up straighter. "What did you find?"

"Nothing."

Ben exhaled loudly. "She's clean?"

"I didn't say that. I said there's nothing to find on your girl past the day she stepped foot in Ivy Springs over a year ago."

"She's using an alias." Ben was surprised...that he actually wasn't surprised by Luke's discovery. He'd known Charlotte was hiding something, so the fact that she wasn't using her real name made sense.

"You have a photo of her? I can run her through facial recognition software to see if I can find an ID."

"I don't, but it doesn't matter. I'll take it from here. Thanks, Luke."

"I shouldn't have to say this to you, but it's never a good sign when someone lies about who they are."

"Which is what I do all the time." Ben settled back against the seat, defeat washing over him.

"That's not what I meant, dumbass. Look, be careful, okay? You're a sucker for a girl in trouble, especially one who's hot. Don't let her get one over on you."

"She's not like that."

"You don't know what she's like," Luke countered. "That's the point."

"I can't walk away, man. She needs help. I have no doubt she's using an alias because she's hiding from something or someone who has her scared. No one should have to live terrified."

"I agree, but until you know for sure that's what's going on, you need to keep your guard up."

"Yeah, okay. I know. You're right. I can't lose perspective. I'll be careful."

"Good. Keep your head on a swivel and reach out if you need us there."

The call ended, but Ben's tumultuous thoughts had just begun spinning. Several minutes passed before Ben reminded himself he needed to get moving. He secured the hair samples in plastic bags he kept in his lunch cooler, and he managed to find a marker in the glove box to label the two samples. He had enough time to grab food and a shower before the Atlas Security operative showed up at the Skyline.

He went through the motions of ordering at a fast-food drive-thru window, paying with cash, and heading back to the motel. Out of habit, he sought out Charlotte's car in the parking lot, but it was gone, as was Wally's vehicle. He suspected Wally and Mona knew the truth behind Charlotte's secrecy, and he was tempted to question them under the guise of wanting to help. But more than he wanted to know the truth, he wanted to hear that truth from Charlotte directly.

He just had to figure out a way to convince her to trust him with her secrets.

CHAPTER ELEVEN

Charlotte squeezed the throw pillow tight against her chest. Her mouth pressed against the scalloped edge, her breath bouncing off the fabric to warm her face. The lamp on the end table beside her cast a yellow glow that once felt warm but now felt eerie. The images on the television screen flickered, holding her enraptured.

Music swelled to a heart-pounding crescendo. She sank deeper against the couch cushions as if they would cocoon her in a shield. The actress on the streaming movie moved with stealth precision, her head turning one way and then the other. The heroine's tension was felt through the screen, and Charlotte heard her own heart thundering in her ears.

A knock sounded out of nowhere, and Charlotte jolted hard enough to fling the throw pillow to the other send of the sofa. Her palm rested over her heart as she struggled to calm herself. She realized the knock was to her own door and caused a streak of fear to rise within her stronger than anything her suspenseful movie conjured.

The knock came again, and she rose slowly, padding on quiet feet to the door. Her hand gripped the baseball bat she kept propped in the corner. She peered through the peephole. Once her eyes adjusted to the darkness outside, she recognized the imposing figure standing on the landing. Hastily releasing the locks, she pulled open the door and froze under Ben's intense stare.

"Hi." He managed to look sheepish as his eyes swept her from head to toe and back.

She was suddenly aware of how she must look. Her hair was pulled back and held in a short ponytail by a black elastic. Her lounge pants were a faded black, and her oversized T-shirt was stained with the spaghetti sauce she had for dinner. She was certain her breath smelled of the garlic that seasoned the bread she'd eaten, and with no makeup on her face, every blemish and freckle was exposed to his scrutiny.

She peered around him, half expecting Ms. Miller to be nearby.

"She saw me from the window when I got out of the Tahoe."

Feeling a little disconcerted that he read her mind so easily, she fixed her gaze in the middle of his chest. It occurred to her to give him a proper greeting, but she was too surprised to see him to think of one.

"What are you doing here?"

His finger nudged her chin, raising her head until their eyes met. "I wanted to see you."

Warmth spread through her, and she nervously stepped back. "Come in."

Once he was inside, she closed the door and realized she still held the bat. Ben raised a brow as she placed it back in its usual spot. She shrugged.

"We don't get many visitors at this time of night."

"I'm sorry. I should have called first."

Charlotte shook her head. "No, it's fine. It's, uh…is everything all right? I mean, not that I'm not happy to see you, but you seem… different."

He ran a hand through his hair, and Charlotte was fascinated with how the waves fell back into place, giving him a roguish appearance.

"It's been a long day." His tone sounded sad, tugging at her heart.

"Do you want to talk about it?"

Ben shook his head. "Not really."

Charlotte shook off her surprise and pointed over to the sofa just as a scream pealed from the television. Seeing the heroine fighting the killer drew her focus. She fully faced the screen, her arms wrapped around her middle. A gasp escaped her throat when the assailant's knife narrowly missed plunging into the heroine's side. A low chuckle reminded her she wasn't alone. Charlotte's cheeks flushed as she glanced at a smiling Ben.

"I'm guessing that's the reason you answered the door armed with a baseball bat," he teased.

"I don't even know why I started watching it. I thought it was a feel-good romantic movie, but then the love interest turned out to be a serial killer. Then he started stalking her, and she was getting closer to figuring out who he was. Anyway, I don't usually watch thrillers like that, but by the time I realized the kind of movie it was, I was too invested to turn it off."

"Well, then, don't let me stop you from seeing it how it ends."

"No, it's fine. We can watch something else. A comedy maybe. Something to help you take your mind off your long day."

Ben stepped closer and took her hand. His palm was deliciously rough against her skin. He led her over to the sofa and lightly pushed her to sit. When he joined her, he left little space between them. His arm draped over her shoulders, pulling her against his side. Then he focused on the screen, leaving her to wonder what just happened.

But then the action of the movie pulled her in once more. She clutched her pillow and burrowed into Ben's side, feeling protected and less afraid by the suspense of the movie. The heroine escaped the clutches of the serial killer only to receive a blow to her head that scrambled her memory. The action flowed, and Charlotte used the lull in suspense to explain the premise to Ben. She had no idea if he cared what was happening, but he humored her.

The movie reached its climax, and Charlotte stopped pretending she wasn't invested in the takedown of the bad guy. She coached the heroine on outsmarting the serial killer, and she cheered when the killer was arrested and the heroine shared a steamy kiss with the new love interest.

"That was great," she said enthusiastically, only to find Ben watching her with a bemused look on his face. "You didn't like it, did you?"

"Maybe if I'd seen it from the beginning. But I liked watching you enjoy it so much."

She snorted. "You mean you hope you don't have to watch another movie with me. I get carried away when I watch movies. I can't help it. I've always been that way."

"I don't mind it. We can watch another one if you want. Having someone who gets into them only makes it more fun to watch."

"We can watch another movie, or we can talk about what brought you to my doorstep."

She didn't quite believe he wanted to see her or spend time with her. There was something bothering him. She sensed it, and she had a bad feeling that whatever it was might somehow involve her.

"Movie," he chose.

"Okay. Well, can I get you anything? Some popcorn? Something to drink? All I have is soda, water, and juice, though."

"Water is fine. Thank you."

She rounded the counter that separated the kitchen area from her living area and retrieved two bottles of water from the refrigerator. When she looked back, Ben had moved to stand by a shelf where she displayed a few photos. They were the only hint of her past she kept, but they tied to her childhood and not the trouble she found as an adult. He reached for a snapshot that she had in a silver frame she'd found for a couple of dollars at a thrift store.

She studied his face as he stared at the picture. His expression was unreadable, and she wondered what held him transfixed. The photo was a shot of her with her parents before they died. Only five years old, she sat on the hood of her father's car with her parents standing on either side of her, holding on to her so she didn't slide off. Her smile was awkward, too wide and frozen in the middle of saying *cheese*.

Her parents, though, looked wonderful. Both were dressed casually and appropriate for the summertime weather. Their smiles were wide and happy, their eyes sparkling with life. It's how she preferred to remember them. Vibrant, in love with each other, in love with her.

"Here's your water," she said as she approached, holding the bottle out to him.

Ben didn't move. One hand held the frame firmly while the other traced the photo along the glass.

"Ben. What's wrong?"

Goosebumps rose on her skin, and she had a radical thought that maybe she misjudged him. He was acting strangely, and lately, she was suspicious of strange behavior.

"Ben. You're freaking me out. Why are you looking at my picture like that?"

He finally turned the force of his gaze on her. The molten chocolate of his eyes swirled with questions and confusion. He pointed to the frame while keeping her ensnared in his stare.

"This is you?"

"Well, the little girl is me. The adults are my parents. Now it's your turn to answer a question. Why are you looking at the picture like that?"

He looked thunderstruck. "You're not Charlotte Redding, are you?"

One bottle of water slipped from her hand and landed with a light thud against the carpet.

"What?" she whispered.

He held the picture up as if comparing it to how she looked today. Suddenly he was in front of her, crowding her space, and she sucked in a startled breath.

"Holy hell. It *is* you."

Charlotte backed up a couple of steps. "I think maybe you'd better tell me exactly who you are, or you can get out of my apartment right now."

He placed the picture on an end table and held his hands up to show he meant her no harm. "I'm sorry. I know you're confused, but bear with me a second. Please."

She wasn't sure she wanted to hear what he had to say, but she found herself nodding anyway.

"Do you remember around the time this picture was taken, maybe later in the year, you helped a kid in your class? A boy with a terrible stutter who was bullied."

Charlotte felt her legs weaken. She did remember. He had been a short, skinny boy who kept to himself. He never spoke, and the teacher never called on him to answer a question or read aloud in class. It wasn't until she heard the cruel teasing that she even knew the boy stuttered.

She stared at Ben with a mixture of awe and suspicion. "How could you possibly know that?"

"You went right up to the bullies and put yourself between them and the boy. Then you proceeded to yell at them. You gave them shit for how they treated him, and then you called them out on all the things that were wrong with them. Thumb-sucker, bed-wetter, couldn't read, couldn't throw a ball, whatever you thought of. You made one of them cry, but they all walked away and left the boy alone after that."

She recalled that day vividly as he spoke, each word out of his mouth describing exactly what happened. Except for one thing he did not mention. Before that day, she had been well-liked by her classmates. She'd been invited to play dates and birthday parties. One little boy even asked her to be his girlfriend, a request that had her scrunching up her nose in disgust and telling the boy she would never have a boyfriend because boys were gross.

After that day, after she did the right thing as her parents taught her to do, she was no longer popular at school. The other kids ignored her. They didn't tease the boy anymore, but neither did they want anything to do with her. The invitations stopped coming. She went from being a favorite in her class to being a nobody.

She'd forgotten about that time of her life. Her family had moved a year later, and her parents had died a short time after that. She was placed in a foster home that was adequate at best. Her foster parents provided the essentials and stayed on her to get good grades and be well-behaved. But once she turned eighteen, they told her she had to move out on her own, so they'd have room to take in another foster child.

Then, with the turn her life had taken the last few years, memories of that little boy had disappeared into the deep recesses of her mind.

"I'm not sure how you can possibly know any of that."

She was freaking out. He was smiling serenely, his dark eyes turning into warm, molten chocolate.

"Because the little boy's name was Ben. And yours was Paige."

Her jaw dropped, and her head flew up to cover her open mouth. She backed up until her legs bumped against the sofa, and she fell to the cushions. Craning her neck, she stared up at the handsome man, searching for signs of the boy she once knew.

When no one else in her class wanted to be her friend, the little boy had been. He was quiet unless he was with her. His stutter made his words hard to understand, but when he was with her, his stutter wasn't so bad. He made her laugh. He taught her to fish. She taught him to play Go Fish and climb a tree.

Her heart had broken when she left him behind, and she mourned the loss of their friendship for months after her family moved. But that had been more than two decades ago. Could it be that fate brought that same boy to her doorstep at a time when it was too dangerous for her to admit who she was?

"I'm not—"

Charlotte jerked when Ben's cell phone rang. He swore vehemently as he pulled it out of his pocket. One glance at the screen, and he silenced it. Kneeling beside her, he lightly took her hand in his. His touch was electric, and she almost pulled away. Then his phone rang again.

"Ignore it," he commanded impatiently, but she shook her head.

"You should answer it. I'm not the girl you're thinking of."

"You are. Paige, I recognize you from the picture."

She shook her head even harder "No. My name is Charlotte. Please, Ben. Let this go. Answer your phone."

The ringing stopped only to begin again immediately. Ben swore again and pushed to his feet. He stepped into the kitchen to answer the call. She barely registered his side of the conversation as the weight of what just happened sank in.

He knew who she was. Her very survival hinged on being anonymous, invisible. Only Wally and Mona knew the truth, or at least part of it. They were the only ones who could know. The more people she told, the more she risked her safety. She'd given up everything just to stay alive, and one chance encounter with a man she'd only known for a short time as a boy might ruin everything.

"I can't...No, it's not...what...what do you mean...are you shitting me..."

Ben's voice continued to rise, and she couldn't tell if he was angry or shocked or frustrated. It didn't matter. She needed him to go, and if whatever the caller was telling him helped to make that happen, then it didn't matter what was going on. She needed to be alone to think about what her next move should be.

"Now? But..."

Charlotte glanced over her shoulder at him. He paced the small space behind the counter, his hand running through his hair. Finally, he mumbled something she didn't understand and ended the call. When he turned his stare on her, she saw he was conflicted.

"Paige—"

"Charlotte," she insisted. "My name is Charlotte Redding. I'm not that little girl. I'm a housekeeper at a small-town motel, and that's all you need to know about me."

Anger flickered in his eyes, and she braced herself in case he took that out on her. Instead, he stomped toward the door, threw it open, and gave her one last look.

"I have to go, but we're not done. I know exactly who you are, and if you think I'm going to walk away without knowing why you're hiding and afraid, you're damn wrong."

The door slammed closed behind him, and Charlotte allowed the tears to fall until sobs overtook her.

CHAPTER TWELVE

Ben stood in the cloak of darkness, watching as the chief of police issued an arrest warrant to Mark Hanson. Keeping a safe distance away, he was close enough to see Hanson's face illuminated by the light spilling from inside the house. The man blustered and fought against the officers handcuffing his hands behind his back. An officer read Hanson his rights, and the man sputtered, insisting there was a mistake.

When he demanded to know their proof, the Chief stepped in front of the man. He motioned for a couple of officers to move inside as he shared with Hanson the charges against him. Kidnapping, child endangerment, fraud. What the Chief didn't say, but what Ben knew, was that Hanson was facing federal charges as well. FBI agents were on their way to Ivy Springs to question him.

Ben itched to be on the man's doorstep. He wanted to look Hanson in the face and watch the other man as he realized Ben was the reason his crimes were discovered. His anger barely in check, Ben stood with his arms crossed over his chest. He was aware of his brothers surrounding him. They arrived in town just as the LEOs rallied to take Hanson down. The Chief agreed to let the Legends watch the arrest as long as they didn't interfere and kept a reasonable distance away.

A hand slapped down on his shoulder. "You okay, man?" Jackson asked.

Ben didn't answer. The officers came outside with Caleb sandwiched between them. The little boy sobbed, his body shaking all over, and Ben felt his heart break. The boy's world was falling apart around him, and he was powerless to stop it. Ben knew that feeling all too well.

"Ben."

"I'm not okay," he finally answered Jackson. "Someone should have done something before now. How did everyone have missed it? How could no one realize that he wasn't who he said he was?"

"You did," Easton said. "You knew something was off with that guy. It's because you kept hunting for the truth that the little boy is away from that guy."

"Then why don't I feel better about it?"

"Because it's a shit situation. But Hanson's going down. The cops have what they need to put him away. And we can make sure the kid gets what he needs to deal with it. We don't have to walk away now that the case is closed," Luke reminded him.

Hanson started shouting after Caleb, but it wasn't the loving reassurance of a parent comforting a child. He yelled for Caleb to keep his mouth shut. He told the little boy that he'd regret it if he talked to anybody. The officers hurried Caleb to a squad car and sped away before Hanson caused any more damage with his words.

Ben never took his eyes from the scene until a separate squad car drove away with the Chief and Hanson inside. The rest of the officers stayed at the house, collecting anything that could strengthen the case against Hanson.

"I never expected this," Ben murmured, knowing his brothers would hear him.

"None of us did," Jackson returned. "We should go. You'll have to give a statement to the cops."

Ben allowed his brothers to pull him along as they headed back to his Tahoe. He didn't argue when Easton offered to drive. He was too distracted to be behind the wheel. Though he wanted to be alone, or better yet back at Charlotte's apartment, he was grateful to have his brothers join him in closing the case.

"I can't believe the DNA test came back so fast," he said as they headed toward the police station.

"It didn't," Luke told him.

Ben shifted in his seat to stare at Luke in the back seat. His eyes adjusted to the limited light, but he barely made out his brother's form. "What are you talking about?"

"It wasn't the DNA. You know that DNA tests don't come back that fast. It was the picture you called me about."

Jackson snorted. "It was dumb luck."

Ben looked from one brother to the other. "Okay, I need to hear the whole story."

"I got to thinking about what you said with Hanson getting the baby from a surrogate or from an affair. So I used facial recognition software to find a familial match to certain facial characteristics in Caleb's picture. Or I guess I should say Dalton," Luke explained.

"Dalton Sims," Ben said quietly, still not believing what they uncovered.

Jackson picked up the story. "His parents live in Randolph, Missouri. His mother was shopping with him and his baby sister. The sister was only a few months old at the time, and Dalton was four. The missing child report said that a strange woman started getting too close to the sister, and their mother was distracted trying to keep the woman away from her baby. Someone, probably Hanson, snatched Dalton while his mother was preoccupied by the woman, who was probably Delia Hanson, or whatever their real names are."

"Dalton's mother runs a non-profit foundation providing aid to families of missing children. They've helped to find something like eighty or so missing kids," Luke said. "In raising money for the foundation, Ms. Sims shares her story of how Dalton was abducted.

His picture is even on the Foundation's website. Not only did the software hit on a familial match with Mr. Sims, it matched with Dalton's pic on the website. We pieced everything together from there."

"So rather than adopting a child, Hanson and his wife stole a toddler? And not the baby?"

Easton joined the conversation. "We think they were trying to take the baby, but Ms. Sims realized what they were doing and kept them from getting too close. We think they took Dalton because they couldn't get to the baby."

"We don't know Hanson's real identity yet. They'll run his fingerprints when they book him, and between that and the DNA test Atlas Security is running, we'll figure out who he is," Jackson said.

"Caleb's real — or rather Dalton's real parents. Have they been notified?" Ben asked.

"Alex offered to break the news. He's flying the family from Missouri to Ivy Springs in the company jet. They'll drive in from the Atlanta airport and probably be here in the morning. They seem like solid people. Maddy Sims' work with the foundation is amazing, and David Sims makes a decent living as an insurance agent. The sister, Amelia, is almost six now," Jackson told him.

"Wow. She was so young when Dalton was abducted, she probably doesn't even remember him." Ben's head started to ache when he pictured what the coming months held in store for the Sims family.

"Try not to think about what's coming," Easton told him. "This family is whole again. That's a big deal."

Ben nodded. "Has anyone told our client? If she hadn't insisted something was wrong, we wouldn't have discovered the truth."

"Reagan's going to call the teacher in the morning and let her know we've closed the case. Once you've given your statement to the police, you can pack up your shit and head home with us," Jackson said.

And just like that, Ben's thoughts returned to Charlotte — to Paige. Once he realized the young girl named Paige and the woman named Charlotte were the same person, he'd been piecing together similarities between the two. The same unusual eyes, but with more gray in them now than when they were kids. The same blond hair that was short and wavy now, versus long and shiny then. The same smile, though adult Paige had all her teeth while child Paige had one or two missing.

She had denied it, but not before she'd let her guard slip, telling him he was right. Paige was pretending to be someone else, and he wanted to know why.

"I'm going to stay in town a few more days. I have some unfinished business."

Easton took his eyes off the road long enough to glance at his brother. "Unfinished business? Yeah, right. What's her name?"

"Charlotte Redding," Luke supplied. "Or at least that's the name she's going by."

"Her name is Paige."

Luke leaned forward. "How did you find out her real name? Did she tell you?"

Ben turned his attention to the passing scenery out his window. "She didn't have to. I know her. Or knew her, a long time ago."

"If you knew who she was, why did you have me run a background on her?"

"I didn't find out for sure who she was until tonight. I knew her when we were kids. Before English and you guys came into my life. It's been over twenty years since we've seen each other."

"Are you serious?" Easton exclaimed. "What are the odds?"

"Evidently better than average," Ben replied dryly.

"Strange that you'd run into her again when she's in trouble," Luke interjected.

"What kind of trouble?" Easton questioned.

Ben frowned. "I don't know. After she got over the shock that I knew who she really was, she stuck to her story. Told me she wasn't who I thought she was. She threw me out of her apartment. You guys called about Hanson, and I had to leave."

"What's your next move?"

Jackson's question was one Ben had refused to considered until now. With his case — the very reason he came to Ivy Springs — cracking wide open, he'd had to walk away when every fiber of his body screamed for him to stay, to find out the truth, to reassure her that she was safe with him.

"I don't know," Ben finally replied. "I can't force her to trust me, and if I don't know what's going on, I don't know how I can help."

Easton scoffed. "Just charm her like you always do when we need people to open up. You never have trouble with that."

"I don't want to pretend with her. She's afraid to trust people, and when she figures out that I haven't been completely upfront with everybody, she's going to shut me out even more."

"So charm someone she knows." Jackson leaned forward. "Get someone she does trust on your side before you offer her your help. But I have to ask. You sure it's a good idea to get involved in what she has going on? You may not like what you find out."

Ben sighed. "I owe her. You guys remember what I was like when I came to live with you. The kids at school, my own family… hell, just about everyone in my life then made me feel worthless. Except for her. Even at six years old, she was fierce. I had never known anyone like her then or since. I really thought I was going to disappear when her family moved from Fire Creek. She was the only person who gave a shit about me. But then I met Gish and you guys. I haven't thought of her much over the years, but I've never forgotten her."

"So this is you paying back a favor? Nothing more?"

Ben opened his mouth to respond to Luke, but the words of agreement refused to pass from his throat. His brothers may not understand his connection to a woman who was both a friend and a stranger, but he wouldn't ignore it.

"Your silence says it all," Easton drawled. "She's your Bailee. Am I right?"

None of them had thought Easton would marry and settle down when he enjoyed the attention of various women he met at the bar or as he went about his life. Same with Jackson and Luke, who never expressed any interest in starting a family of their own. Their experiences with family weren't worth repeating, and though they found acceptance in the makeshift family they created, they had no idea what it took to create the fairytale happily ever after with a wife, kids, and the proverbial house with a picket fence.

But Jackson met English's daughter, who went from not wanting anything to do with her biological father and the boys he chose to raise over her, to marrying one of those boys and building an unorthodox relationship with her father. Luke met Melody, who was raised in a loving family, but through her job as a paralegal, had seen the worst of what humanity could do. And Easton met Bailee, a woman who showed him they could truly have it all.

Ben had no idea if Paige was *it* for him or not, but he refused to believe it was an accident that the grownup version of him met the grownup version of her at this point in their lives. She needed help. He was qualified to provide it. And then they would be free to get to know each other as the adults they were now. They could walk away with a renewal of the friendship they had as children. Or they could walk away with more. Ben would be lying if he said the thought didn't appeal to him.

"You need us to stick around too?" Jackson asked before Ben found the words to respond.

"I can't ask you to do that. Not when I have no clue what's going on with her and even if she's going to be open to my help."

"Sure you can," Luke drawled. "We're Legends. It's what we do."

Ben felt his grin split his face. "Damn straight. But no, I think I got this. You guys hold the fort down at home, and once we wrap up the mess with Hanson, I can focus on Paige. I'll find a way to convince her to trust me."

"Atta boy," Easton teased as he turned the Tahoe into the parking lot at the police station. He killed the engine just as daybreak started to peek through the darkness. "If anybody can get through to her, it's you. But if you screw it up, just call me. I may be married with a kid, but women still find me irresistible. Just ask Bailee."

As if they practiced the maneuver, Jackson, Luke, and Ben threw out their fists connecting with Easton's back, shoulder, and arm with punches meant to be good-natured while still packing some heat behind them.

"Hey!" Easton rubbed the spot on his upper arm. "Punch me all you want. It won't change the truth."

Easton scooted out of the Tahoe before they punched him again. Ben and his other brothers followed suit. As they walked as a formidable group into the police station, Ben's expression turned serious. Even with all the grief his brothers gave each other, Ben was glad to have them there as he closed the book on this case.

CHAPTER THIRTEEN

When she fell into a fitful sleep at three in the morning, she was Charlotte Redding of Ivy Springs, housekeeper by day, recluse by night.

When she woke the next morning, feeling exhausted and frightened, she was Paige Childers, a woman without a place to land.

Paige stood in front of the mirror over her bathroom sink, staring at her reflection, feeling like a stranger was looking back at her. Her eyes were a smoky gray reflecting her sadness, red-rimmed and swollen from the tears she never thought would end last night. Her skin always had the look of someone in need of a day in the sunshine, but this morning, the creamy complexion was washed out. She looked ill and felt like it with the way her heart felt battered and bruised.

Her alarm had jolted her awake as it did every morning she worked at the motel. Though all she wanted to do was roll over and forget the world existed outside her apartment door, she forced herself to go through the motions she completed each day. Brushed her teeth. Showered. Dried her hair only to secure the shorter locks away from her face with a bobby pin or hair tie.

She made her bed before dressing in her black uniform. Sitting on the edge of the mattress, she pulled on her comfortable shoes. Then her body felt heavy, her stomach rolled with nausea, and her temples began to ache. The idea of standing, much less going to work, felt impossible. Though she knew the questions it would raise and the visitors it would bring to her door, she fired off a quick text to Wally.

Sick. Won't be in today. Contagious. Talk to you later.

She doubted it would be enough to stop Wally, Mona, or even Birdie from checking on her in concern. But it bought her enough time to fall back against the mattress, pull her knees to her chest, and close her eyes to the pain that wouldn't let her go.

Since discovering who Ben truly was, memories that she'd believed were forgotten resurfaced. She indulged in them as she lay in a fetal position. She recalled the day she had to tell her old friend she was leaving for good. At six years old, she didn't understand why her family had to move from Fire Creek. Something about her father receiving a promotion that required them to move to Biloxi, Mississippi. She thought it to be a world away instead of a few hours' worth of driving.

She had met Ben at their usual place to hang out and play. It was in the wooded area by the neighborhood park. A copse of trees hid a grassy field under the shade of its limbs. It was a perfect spot to play pretend, to have a picnic, or to tell your best friend you weren't going to see them anymore.

She'd been the first to reach their clubhouse, as they called the open area shielded by trees on all sides. When Ben showed up, she'd been shocked to find his clothes dirty and torn, his hair in need of a comb, and his lip bloody and swollen. The conversation she dreaded having was forgotten when her rage rose to a blinding intensity.

Of course, she didn't show her anger to Ben. She marched right up to him, touched a soft hand to his cheek, and said one word. "Who?"

He'd covered her hand with his but hung his head low. "D-d-doesn-n-n't m-m-m-mat-t-t-ter."

Ben's stutter was severe, but for some reason, when it was just the two of them, it wasn't as pronounced. Most of the time, Paige hardly noticed, so the fact that he tripped over his words painfully told her all she needed to know.

"I swear Mitch Cason is going to regret messing with you. One day, when you've had enough, you're going to beat him black and blue. Maybe even punch out his front tooth so he talks with a lisp. I saw that on a cartoon once."

That had brought a faint smile to his lips. She smiled too until she remembered what she had to tell him. She turned her back to him then, sighing with the weight of the adult conversation she had to have.

"You're going to have to start doing that, you know," she had said while trying to build her confidence to tell him about her leaving. "Standing up for yourself. You can't let everyone walk all over you. You're better than that. You're better than all of them."

"N-n-n-not y-y-y-y-you."

She whirled back around, "Yes, you are. You are so much better than me. You're strong and brave and smart and kind. You're good at fishing, and you're the fastest runner at school. You know more about science than Ms. Maxwell does. And that box you made me to keep my seashells in? I couldn't do that. No way. So stop putting yourself down. I won't always be here to tell you this stuff, so you have to remember it."

"W-w-what d-d-d-do you m-m-mean?"

Paige remembered the dread filling the pit of her stomach when he caught her slip. She almost brushed it off and made it seem like her words had no hidden meaning. But she couldn't. She was running out of time.

"My family is moving away. Daddy got a new job, and we have to go."

He was so still she wondered if he heard her. When he finally spoke, she felt like she'd destroyed his world.

"When?" No stutter. Just quiet calm, like he prepared himself for this moment all along.

"Two weeks. Daddy's leaving tomorrow to find us a place to live. Momma said we'll pack up and go later."

"T-take me t-too."

"What?"

"D-don't l-leave me behind. P-please."

She didn't know much about his life outside of school, but she knew enough. No father. A mother who didn't love him. Days when he went hungry or dirty or both. Times when he camped out at their clubhouse because it was nicer than going home. He lived a life she couldn't imagine. Her parents loved her, cared for her, and gave her whatever she needed and other things she wanted.

She remembered the lump that grew in her throat until she thought she would choke. She swallowed it down, her voice thick when she answered.

"I already asked. They said no."

Her tears had flowed freely then, and he cried some too. They sat in their clubhouse until Paige knew she had to go home or get in trouble. They spent every moment together from that day until she left Fire Creek in the rearview mirror. She never saw or heard from him again, but sometimes in the years that followed, she wondered what happened to him.

Her mind hardly reconciled the scrawny little boy she once loved to the grown man who both intimidated and excited her. When they were kids, she felt like she was the one protecting him from the world. Now he offered to protect her. He wanted her trust.

But he didn't how deep her trouble went. Anyone within her circle of trust was put at risk. She'd had to place Wally in that circle, and Mona by default. Ms. Miller only knew enough to not ask too many questions, but she had no idea the depth of the danger Paige was in if she didn't remain hidden.

Paige didn't realize she fell asleep until she jerked awake sometime later to her cell phone ringing. She twisted her head to follow the sound until she spotted her phone where she left it on her dresser. The call ended by the time she picked up her phone, and she saw a couple of missed calls and incoming texts flashing on the screen. The calls were from Ms. Miller and Wally with no voicemails. Not surprising since they hated talking to recordings. The texts were from Mona, asking how she was and if she needed anything.

She dropped her phone to the mattress. The calls and the messages wouldn't stop. Eventually they'd show up on her doorstep. They'd want to know what was wrong. She could refuse to tell them, and they would respect her privacy. She couldn't do that. They had been too kind and supportive for her to shut them out now.

So she wouldn't. She would explain the incredible twist of fate that brought the boy she once loved back into her life at a time when her life wasn't her own. Maybe they could help her figure out how to drive Ben away because she was sure he wouldn't let her go until he knew everything she kept hidden. If she tried to leave, as she had before, he would follow her. She was as certain of that as she was the next breath she drew.

She stood and started getting ready to face her friends, praying answers would miraculously come to her before she had to face Ben Weston again.

CHAPTER FOURTEEN

Paige dropped her keys into her bag as her feet walked the familiar path from the parking lot to the lobby of the Skyline Motel. She'd been surprised to find the weather pleasant enough for her to shed the jacket she wore. The sun beamed on her, a contrast to the dark mood she was in. She threw open the door and stepped inside, her steps faltering when she heard familiar voices talking low from the direction of the seating area.

When Wally and Ben noticed her, they stood. From their expressions, she figured they had been talking about her, and the thought bothered her. She pinned Ben with a glare.

"You told him." The accusation dripped with disdain.

"Not exactly."

Paige rolled her eyes. "Stop talking in riddles."

Wally looked from Ben to her in confusion. "Charlotte, honey, I don't know what you're talking about, but all he said was that you and he knew each other when you were kids. That was right before you came in."

She took a deep breath and released it slowly. "I was coming to talk to you about that myself. I didn't expect Ben to beat me to it."

"Come over here and sit down. You look about ready to drop." Wally motioned for her to take the empty spot on the couch next to where Ben had been sitting.

With one last glare at Ben, she moved to sit in an empty chair instead. "I'm fine. Just tired. I'm sorry you had to get Betsy to cover for me."

Wally waved off her apology. "It does that woman good to have something to do. You sure you're okay?"

She nodded. "It was a rough night, but I'm fine. I do have something I want to talk to you about. Alone."

She stared at Ben pointedly, but he seemed unfazed by her ire.

"We can talk," Wally agreed. "But I think you need to hear what Ben has to say first.

Her eyes snapped to her boss. "Wally, I don't—"

"In this case, I think you should talk to him. Trust me on this. I've never steered you wrong before."

She started to protest again, but Wally stood and walked into his office before she uttered a word. She stared after him, mainly because she didn't want to face Ben when it was just the two of them.

"Paige..."

"Don't call me that." She turned back but couldn't meet his eyes. Her hands settled on her lap, and she stared at them.

"It's your name."

She shook her head. "Not anymore."

"And why is that?"

She lifted her eyes to meet his. "You think because you convinced Wally to take your side that I'm going to tell you everything? Believe me. You don't want to know."

"You're wrong about that, but I understand why you don't want to talk. We don't know each other. Not really. But I hope you'll listen. I have a lot I want to tell you. All I ask is that you hear me out. Then if you want me to leave, I will."

Her eyes narrowed as a realization dawned on her. "You have secrets too."

"Something like that."

"I don't want to know, Ben. I can't. What I'm dealing with...it's too big for me to take on your secrets too."

"That's just it. My shoulders are big enough to carry mine and yours. I can ease your burden."

Paige shook her head. "No one wants to carry mine."

"Like I said, hear me out and then decide."

Her head told her to say no, but her heart wasn't in it. She wanted to hear what Ben had to say. She wanted to know more about the man he was now. What had happened in his life since they had known each other? Why was he so anxious to help her? What secrets did he have that would make a difference to her situation now?

"I'll listen."

Ben didn't bother to hide his relief that she agreed. "Is there somewhere more private we can go?"

She nodded. "Come on."

She didn't bother knocking before leading him through Wally's office. She had no doubt that her boss had been listening, and she refused to look his way when he likely watched her with a knowing expression. Stepping through the back exit, she headed to the grassy area beside the back parking lot. Though it was out in the open, no one would disturb them. She sat at the picnic table and waited for Ben to join her. She kept silent, giving him the chance to say what he wanted to say.

"I'm not sure where to start."

Paige guffawed. "I know the feeling. I'm still trying to reconcile that you are the boy I knew when I was six."

He grinned. "A lot has happened since we hung out at the clubhouse. It's still there, you know."

"It is?"

"I still live in Fire Creek. I go by there sometimes. Not a lot. It's hard, even now, to go there by myself. That was always our spot. It wasn't the same after you moved."

"That was so long ago."

"It was not long after that when I went to live with Gish and my brothers. Everything I told you about them was true. You already knew that my dad was never in my life, and my mom...well, she never wanted me around. One day, she left and never came home. I found out later that she overdosed on heroin, and since she had no ID on her, the city labeled her a Jane Doe. No one knew to come for me.

"I was scared of what was going to happen to me when she didn't come home, so I never told anyone about it. I pretended everything was okay, and whenever anyone came by the apartment looking for her, I made excuses about why she wasn't there. I started doing odd jobs for people in the neighborhood and used that money to buy food. I thought I was keeping up the pretense, but my landlord knew. He lived in the building, and when the rent went unpaid, and he stopped seeing my mom around, he figured she'd abandoned me."

Ben placed his arms on top of the picnic table and leaned forward. "My three brothers all came from rough upbringings, and Gish took them in when they had nowhere to go. My landlord told me he knew where my mom was, and he was going to take me to her. Instead, he left me at the bar for Gish to find."

Paige thought she was all cried out, but she felt tears prick the back of her eyes. "I'm sorry. I knew things were bad for you at home, but I had no idea."

"No reason why you would. We were six. We didn't talk about that stuff. Hell, with my stutter, I didn't talk at all if I could help it."

"And now your stutter is gone. It's hard to believe you're the same person."

"I'm not. Living with Gish and my brothers changed my life. There was a woman who worked at the bar...Her name is Becky. She acted more like a mother to me than my own ever did. I wished

Gish would marry her and make it official, but their relationship is a whole other story for another day. Anyway, she helped me learn to control my stutter, and she said with my imagination and my gift for pretending, I should be an actor. My brothers were big into sports. I started acting in plays at school."

Paige smiled. "That's hard to picture. I mean, I always knew you had a fun personality. I just never imagined you'd show that to anyone but me."

"I had the chance to take a theatre scholarship when I graduated from high school. It would have been the only way I could have afforded college because my grades were mediocre at best. I didn't take it, though. My brothers and I decided to follow in Gish's footsteps, so we enlisted in the Army."

She digested that bit of information and felt like there was more to that decision than what he'd told her. She didn't have to wait long for him to enlighten her.

"Remember I said Gish often helped people who needed it?"

She nodded. "That's why he took you and our brothers in."

"And the Becky that I mentioned?"

"Who is like a mother to you."

"Well, Gish had been helping people long before my brothers and I came into the picture. He helped Becky, too. She had an abusive boyfriend who got her hooked on drugs. Gish helped her get clean. He gave her a job at the bar and helped her start a new life. He's helped a lot of people, but he made sure what he did wasn't public knowledge."

She tilted her head, her face twisted in bewilderment. "What are you trying to tell me, Ben?"

"Not many people know this, but I trust that what I tell you is between us and just us." At her nod, he continued. "Gish is a former CIA operative. After he left the Agency, he continued to help people who needed it but couldn't get it any other way. When my brothers and I found out about what he was doing, we decided we wanted to do the same."

"Like you're giving back to someone else because of the people who helped you. They call it paying it forward, I think."

Ben nodded. "Exactly. Our training in the Army and what Gish taught us prepared us to help people in all sorts of situations. Even dangerous situations."

There it was. The bombshell he wanted to drop on her. The proof that she trusted him to help her.

"Ben—"

"Wait, please. Let me say this. We call ourselves the Legends because that's how Gish was known when he was in the CIA. We each own our own business, and when someone reaches out to us, we figure out the best way to help them. We either work together or separately based on what is needed. We've helped people with stalkers, with missing persons…well, you get the idea."

"If you own your own business, why are you working construction?"

"I was here on a case. I was only on the construction crew to get close to our suspect. That's why I had to leave you so suddenly last night. We got what we needed to close the case, and my brothers and I needed to be there for the arrest."

"I guess if I asked about the case, you would tell me, but then you'd have to kill me."

He grinned at her use of spy-inspired humor. "I can tell you some. The arrest makes it public record. A man and his wife kidnapped a little boy because they were unable to have children of their own. This happened five years ago. His wife committed suicide a year ago, and last night the man was arrested for the kidnapping. The little boy is being reunited with his birth family today. There's still a lot to unwrap from all of this, but that's the gist. I came here to investigate the man because he was suspected of abusing the boy. There wasn't any evidence of physical abuse, but from what we've uncovered, there's been emotional and psychological abuse."

She felt her eyes widening the more he shared. "Oh, my God. I don't even know what to say to that. I can't believe that happened here. Ivy Springs is such a quiet town. It's why I stopped here."

"Stopped?"

She hesitated. This was part of her story that she'd shared with people in town, but somehow sharing it with Ben felt like a slippery slope, as if opening up to him about this detail would compel her to tell him all of it. She wasn't sure she was ready to do that. But he could glean this information from Wally if he'd thought to ask, so it didn't make sense for her not to tell him.

"I was on a bus heading to Atlanta. We weren't supposed to stop here, but there was a problem with the bus. It was fixed pretty quick, but I decided to stay behind instead of going to Atlanta. That was over a year ago."

"Let me guess. A fresh start in a new town and a new name."

She shrugged. "Something like that."

"It's more than that," he countered. "The first time we met after I came to town? Aside from the fact that you broke my nose, I saw that you were afraid. You are afraid. You didn't settle in this town. You're hiding here. You're running from something. And don't deny it because I won't believe you. One of my talents is discerning what people are dealing with."

She scowled. "Why do you care what I'm dealing with? You don't owe me anything. It doesn't matter that we once knew each other some twenty-something years ago. It sounds like the reason you came to town has been taken care of. There's nothing keeping you here. Unless you're trying to fulfill some need to be a hero or something. If that's it, forget it. I'm not your charity case."

"Paige—"

Once again, their conversation was interrupted by his phone ringing. She crossed her arms over her chest as she watched him check the screen, frown, and then answer. Whoever was on the other end of the line dominated the conversation, and Ben's face hardened the more he listened. Finally, he ended the call without saying good-bye and pushed to his feet to step over the picnic table's bench seat. He grasped her hand and pulled her up.

"Come on. We'll have to finish this later."

"Wh..." She sputtered as she scrambled after him. "Ben, where are we going?"

He didn't answer, and she had to half-walk, half-run to keep up with his hurried strides. They rounded the side of the motel, and she slammed into his back when he stopped abruptly. She peered around his solid frame and gasped at the spectacle happening in front of the Skyline. News reporters from television networks had cameras on tripods facing away from the motel toward the traffic passing on the street.

She backed away, jerking her hand from his hold. Whipping around on her heel, she ran around the back of the hotel before one of those cameras swung in her direction and ruined everything.

CHAPTER FIFTEEN

"Where is she?"

Ben hadn't meant to come storming into Wally's office at the Skyline Motel like a bull charging an opponent, but when Paige ran from him and disappeared, desperation built within his chest. The motel owner stared at him in shock, but Ben barely noticed since he didn't expect to find his brother also standing in the small office.

Luke stepped in front of him, placing a hand on his brother's chest. The gesture wasn't enough to stop Ben if he'd wanted to keep moving, but it was enough to make him take a breath.

"I thought you went home."

Luke was unfazed by his brother's bark. "Fully intended to until the media vultures descended. They caught the story of Hanson's arrest and have been all over town trying to scoop each other. Some idiot at the construction site tipped them off that you and Hanson butted heads. Since the police won't tell them what's going on, they're hoping you hate the guy enough to do it for them."

Ben blew out an irritated breath. "Yeah. My boss with the construction company called and tipped me off."

Luke nodded. "Jackson and Easton are hanging out at the police station to try to diffuse everything over there. I offered to find you, so we can get the hell out of here."

Ben wasn't shocked that the media showed up. The kidnapping case would grab national headlines. He hadn't expected them to arrive in Ivy Springs so quickly, and he hated that they were trying to expose his connection to the case. The Legends were only successful if they operated under the radar.

"I can't leave without talking to Paige. She ran when she saw the cameras, and I can't find her."

"Haven't seen her, man. You sure it was the cameras she was running from?"

Ben shoved Luke back. "Stop messing around. I have to find her."

Wally stepped around his desk and peered out a side window that faced the parking lot. "Her car's gone."

"She probably went back to her apartment. Distract the press so I can go after her?"

Luke frowned. "Don't you think we have bigger problems to deal with than chasing some girl?"

"Charlotte's not *some* girl," Wally snapped, glaring at Luke before turning his attention to Ben. "I'll think of something to get rid of the media. Don't let her get away from you, son, and don't make me regret trusting you with my girl."

"I won't," Ben promised. "I just wish I could convince her to trust me, too. I can't help if she doesn't talk to me."

"All I know is someone's after her, and whoever it is wants her dead. She's never told us more than that. If I knew the whole story, I'd say so even if she hated me for doing it."

Wally's cell phone rang, and he stepped back to his desk to answer it. "Hold on, son. It's Mona. She may have heard from Charlotte."

After a few minutes, Ben figured from Wally's side of the conversation that Mona did know where Paige was, and he waited impatiently to find out. He was ready to jump out of his skin by the time the older man hung up.

"She's at Mona's shop. It's just down the road, but she's upset. Since Mona's part-time employee is there to cover for her, she is taking Charlotte back to her house. You know where it is. You two go. I'll get rid of the media and head that way."

"Thanks, Wally."

"Come on," Luke said begrudgingly. "I'll drive."

Luke and Wally exited the front of the hotel. Wally yelled for the television crews to disburse off his property, and as he did, he made sure their attention was on him and facing away from Luke's truck. Once the coast was clear, Ben darted from the lobby and slipped into the passenger side. Luke carefully drove out of the parking lot and headed in the direction Ben showed him.

"Wanna tell me why this girl has you twisted in knots?"

Ben didn't because he wasn't sure he knew, but he owed his brothers an explanation of some kind. If he was willing to risk the anonymity of the Legends, they deserved to know why.

"You already know I was bullied a lot as a kid because of my stutter. Well, the first time I met Paige was when she stood up for me. She got all the bullies to back off. She went from being one of the most popular girls in our class to being an outcast because she defended me. She didn't care. She was the only friend I ever had until I came to live with you guys."

Luke took his eyes off the road long enough to see his brother's face. "So this is what? A way to say thank you?"

Ben almost nodded but stopped. "No. That's not what this is. I wanted to help her before I realized she was the same girl I knew back in school. We were six when we were friends before, so when I saw her at the motel, I didn't recognize her. I tried to ask for extra towels, but I scared her so much that she punched me and broke my nose. It was not a common reaction of someone who is caught by surprise. She's deeply afraid."

"But she won't tell you why? Even after you told her about the Legends?"

Ben narrowed his eyes at his brother. "How did you know I told her?"

All of them were careful with whom they told about their work. His brothers had taken a while to open up to their wives about the Legends, and he'd only told Paige that morning.

Luke rolled his eyes as if Ben asked a question he already knew the answer to. "You're risking a lot for this girl."

"I might be wrong, but I believe she's worth it."

"Now that we know who she is, why don't you let me do a deep dive on her? At least make sure she hasn't done anything in the last twenty years that raises red flags."

Ben shook his head. "Is it wrong that I want her to tell me what's going on instead of us digging it up?"

Luke sobered. "No. I don't like not knowing what you're getting yourself into with her, but I get it. You're in love with her."

Ben drew his mouth into a thin line. "What? I'm not in love with her. I haven't seen her in years. I don't know anything about her. We've only spent a little time together since I've been in town."

"You don't realize it yet, but you're in love with her. I just hope she doesn't crush you while you're trying to be her hero."

"Stop saying I'm in love, jackass. That's not what this is, and it's not me wanting to be a hero. I wish you, Easton, and Jackson would realize that. What's wrong with me wanting to help her? If you saw how frightened she is, you'd do the same."

"Sure, I would. But my heart is not involved like yours is. You can swear all day that your concern is the same as what you would feel for any client , but that's bullshit. You're drawn to this girl. I can see it. Why the hell can't you?"

"If it'll make you happy, I'll admit it," Ben shouted. "I'm drawn to her. Can you blame me? She's beautiful. Sweet. Works hard. She deserves to live a life where she's not looking over her shoulder all the time. I believe we can make that happen for her. Am I wrong?"

"Nope. I just want to make sure you're going into this with your eyes wide open. If she's caught your interest, she's gotta be someone special. But she has no idea what you're risking for her. And you have no idea how she feels about you."

"She could hate me, and it doesn't matter. She needs us. We can't walk away. I can't walk away."

"So we don't. But I'm checking her out. It's what we'd do for any client, and I'm not treating her different just because you owe her," Luke warned.

"Fine, but I don't want to know what you find out. I want to hear it from her."

"And if she doesn't tell you?" Luke countered.

"I don't know. I have to believe she will."

Ben pointed out Mona's house, and Luke parked in the driveway in front of the two-car garage.

"Let me do all the talking," Ben cautioned him.

"You do your thing. I'll do mine." Luke reached behind his seat for the backpack that held his laptop. "You go on in. I can work out here, and I'll check in with Jackson and Easton. Call if you need backup."

Ben nodded, squared his shoulders, and walked to the front door. He raised his fist to knock, but the door swung open before he did. Paige stood in front of him, her eyes wide enough for him to see the pale gray of the irises. He'd come ready to plead his case, but her obvious vulnerability had his arguments flying out of his mind. He hated the resignation in her posture as if she was giving up.

"Can we talk?"

Paige shook her head. "There's no point. I saw a news report. There's a lot of attention on you right now. I have to steer clear of that."

"I do too. My brothers want me to head home with them, but I can't. Not until I talk to you."

Ben thought she was going to close the door in his face, but at the last second, she seemed to reconsider. "Okay. You can come in. What about him?"

She tilted her head in the direction of the truck, and Ben glanced over his shoulder at his brother, who was on the phone to who Ben assumed was Jackson or Easton.

"He's my brother. He's going to wait in the truck while we talk if that's okay."

She nodded. "Fine. Come in."

He stepped inside when she moved back. Glancing around Mona's house, he waited for Paige to close the door and lead the way to the living area.

"Where's Mona?"

"She said she's giving us privacy," Paige explained.

"How did she know you would talk to me?"

Paige shrugged and motioned for him to sit. She moved to stand by the window as if too anxious to remain still.

"Mona and Wally think I should trust you. They've never told me to reach out to anyone before, not even the police. But you are different. I'm not sure what you've done to convince them of that, but it worked, whatever it was."

"I wish I knew because I'd try it on you."

She whipped around, her hair flying away from her face. "This isn't a game, Ben. You have reporters wanting to shove TV cameras in your face. Being seen with you might get me killed if I'm caught on video in any way. I wish you'd believe that it's better if I don't say anything."

"I wish you'd believe that I can keep you safe if you'd tell me what I'm keeping you safe from."

Luke's voice interrupted. "He's right."

Paige jerked and backed up until the wall hit her back. Ben wasn't sure why Luke was standing at the back of the room, but he figured it wasn't good. Luke and Paige squared off, swapping intense stares that had Ben wondering if he was witnessing an old-fashioned standoff.

"I'm Luke, Ben's br—"

"His brother. I know. He talks about you and the others a lot."

Luke smirked. "He talks a lot about a lot of things. And you probably feel like he's been lying to you the whole time he's been in town. He had to though, and because he did, a little boy got out of a tough situation. One almost as bad as the situation you're in."

Ben's head whipped around, and he saw her flinch.

"But I never told…How did you…"

"Finding things out is my superpower. Ben wanted to hear things from you, but for me to have his six, I had to know the truth using the tools at my disposal."

She glared at him. "You had no right."

He glared back. "I have every right. He's determined to help you even though you don't want it. I would rather get out of here, but I suppose I owe you for watching out for him when you were kids. And now that I know what you're hiding...well, I don't think I can walk away from you either."

"That's not up to you."

"Shit, lady, just tell him the truth. You need help, and we can give it. You're only wasting time by digging in your heels."

Ben didn't like how heated things were becoming between them. "Luke, it's okay."

Luke nodded, then pierced Paige with a pointed stare. "Stop trying to take this on by yourself. It's too much. You know I'm right."

Ben fought the urge to step in and defend Paige. She handled herself well with his brother, and he was impressed. Luke was impressed too, though he would never let it show. His brother lifted his chin at him before he left through the front door. Ben turned back to see Paige still staring at the spot Luke vacated, tears streaming down her face.

He closed the distance between them. Pulling her against his chest, she sank into his embrace. Sobs shook her body, and he tightened his hold. Her tears soaked his shirt, and he stroked her hair with one hand, hoping the ministrations would comfort her. For once, he had no idea what to say or what to do. He wanted to tell her everything would be all right, but he suspected she wouldn't believe him.

Her sobs subsided, but she stood still in his arms. His hand moved from her hair to her back, sliding up and down until she pulled back. She looked up at him, and he touched her cheek.

"I'm sorry if Luke was too harsh."

She swallowed. "No. It's fine. He's looking out for you, and I can't be hurt by that. I'm glad you have someone in your life now."

He smiled gently. "I have lots of someones like that, but I find it hard to be grateful for them when it seems like they're always interrupting us. If I believed in such things, I'd wonder if the universe was conspiring to keep us from talking."

Paige drew in a shaky breath. "Actually, I think the universe is trying to keep us together despite all the interruptions. I need you to understand something. I want to tell you everything. Believe me, I'm tired of keeping it all in. I'm tired of looking for danger everywhere I turn. But I'm terrified of something happening to you or my friends if I do."

"I do understand, but I promise I can handle it."

She closed her eyes. "God help me, but I believe you."

He dipped his head, so their eyes were on the same level. "Does that mean you'll talk to me?"

She drew in a deep breath, released it, and opened her eyes. "Yes. I'll tell you."

CHAPTER SIXTEEN

Paige rubbed warmth back into her arms. Whenever she thought about the time of her life when she could live as Paige Childers, she felt a chill that lingered no matter what she did. Ben had taken a seat, but she couldn't be still. Moving kept the sadness from settling in her bones.

"You told me what happened to you after I moved away when we were six. I know that has nothing to do with what you want to know, but if it's okay, I'm going to start there. Build up to what's happening now," she began.

"That's fine. I'd like to know that too."

She smiled at him, seeing a glimpse of the gentle boy she once knew. "A few months after we moved to Mississippi, my parents and I were in a car accident. They...died, and I was in the hospital for a couple of days. When I was discharged, I was placed with a foster family, the Walkers. They didn't have children of their own, but they had a couple of other fosters living there when I came. Over the years, they had as many as five fosters at one time. They were nice enough. They made sure we had everything we needed. They were kind. They pushed us to do well in school. But we weren't a family. It felt more like we were tenants renting a room from them."

Her pacing slowed, and she glanced over to see Ben listening intently. "Their rule was that when we turned eighteen and aged out of the system, we were on our own. What we did after that was none of their concern. On my seventeenth birthday, they reminded me of this, and I lived that next year worrying about what I would do when I wasn't living with them anymore.

"My teachers noticed something was wrong, and they asked the guidance counselor to talk to me. I opened up to her. She said my grades were good enough to get a scholarship to college, and she offered to help me with the applications and any housing assistance. She encouraged me to start an extracurricular activity to make more of an impression on my college applications. I joined the student newspaper staff. I sucked at writing articles, though, so they had me take pictures. The sponsor had a camera that he let me use. I wasn't very good, but I read up on photography and taught myself some tricks. I fell in love with it, and my sponsor said he was very impressed with how far I'd come."

She smiled because this part of her past was pleasant. "I got accepted to college, and between scholarships and loans, I was able to live on campus. I studied photography even more and became better at it. I had an instructor give me a nice camera to use. He said it was old, and he didn't need it anymore. That was a lie. He felt sorry for me and knew I couldn't afford to get a camera on my own. I probably should have refused, but I don't regret taking it. Having that camera changed my life.

"My instructor helped me sell some photos to the local newspaper, and I was able to make some extra money. When I graduated, I went to work for a portrait photographer. When he retired, he sold me his equipment, and I ran my own business. I wasn't rich, but I operated in the black. My reputation grew. I had a few regular customers. I had been so afraid of what would happen to me after I turned eighteen, but my life came together better than I hoped."

"You're a photographer," Ben finally said. "That's great, Paige."

"I *was* a photographer. I had to stop. It would make me too easy to find if I kept it up."

Ben's face was a mask of confusion. "Are you in witness protection?"

She uttered a dry chuckle. "Not exactly, but I can see where you would make that assumption. Just bear with me, and I'll explain. I had a client who asked me to take portraits of him and his family at their home. Then he wanted pictures of his house and property. He never explained what he wanted them for, and I didn't ask. There was no reason for me to know that. The job went perfectly. I finished with the portraits, and he loaned me a horse to ride around his property and snap any photos that caught my attention. My foster family had taken us horseback riding a couple of times, so I wasn't unfamiliar with how to ride, and my client gave me a gentle horse. I had the best time. It was late in the spring. The weather was sunny and very warm. Everything was blooming. It was ideal."

Her heart pounded against her chest, and she wrung her hands together to relieve their clamminess. "When I finished, I returned the horse and went to say goodbye. As I was walking to the front door of the main house, I saw my client, Mr. Warner, through these glass patio doors he had in his home office. So instead of walking to the front of the house, I decided to save some time and cut through the patio. I mean, I was just letting him know that I was leaving. I was going to be quick and then be on my way, so I didn't see any harm in it."

She wasn't aware that she started using her hands to illustrate her story, and her arms swung wide as she continued. "I got to the patio door and heard gunshots. Three of them. Mr. Warner fell. I mean, he just hit the floor like a tree being cut down in the woods. He, uh, he was shot in the chest. Twice." Her finger pointed to her chest in the same spot her client had been shot before touching her temple. "Then once in the head. His head had rolled to the side when he fell. His eyes were still open and staring right at me. They were blank. Lifeless. They haunt me."

"Oh, Paige—"

She held up a hand to stop him. "Please. Let me get this out. I remember dropping my camera and my phone because my hands shook so bad. I started screaming, and then I ran. I jumped in my car and drove as fast as I could. Eventually, I made my way to the police station and filed a report. I wasn't able to tell them much. I didn't remember seeing the shooter, and I didn't know Mr. Warner well enough to know who would kill him. I couldn't even tell the police what he needed the photos for."

"Did they offer you police protection?"

She shook her head. "They didn't see a need. The shooter never came after me when I ran. I couldn't give them a lead on who it was. I got the impression that, as far as witnesses go, I was pretty useless. I wish the killer had believed that."

"Did he come after you?"

"Yeah. I was attacked the next day outside my studio. He got me from behind and told me to keep my mouth shut, or I'd regret it. He told me in great detail what he would do to me if I said anything to anyone about what I saw. He wouldn't kill me. He would rape and torture me until I wished I were dead. Just to prove he meant business, he broke my wrist."

"Oh, Paige, I'm—"

She held up a shaky hand to stop him. "No, please. It's hard enough to talk about it. If I stop now, I might not continue."

He simply nodded, and she picked up her story. "The same detective who was assigned to Mr. Warner's murder case came to the hospital while they were setting my wrist. I filed a report, but it wasn't going to do any good since I had my back to him the whole time. The detective promised to ask for extra patrols around my house and studio as a precaution. He drove me home after I was discharged.

"The killer was waiting for me at my house. As soon as I stepped inside, he grabbed me. He slapped his hand over my mouth so I couldn't scream. I kicked him. It took a couple of tries, but I finally got him good enough that he dropped his hand. I screamed. The detective hadn't left yet. He was talking to one of the patrols that had come by, so he heard me scream. He busted in, and the killer shot him and the patrolmen with him. I ran and hid in a tree on a neighbor's property a couple of doors down from my place. I didn't climb down until I heard sirens stopping on my street.

"The officers weren't killed, thank God. The district attorney insisted on putting me in protective custody. It was crazy. I couldn't identify the man, but as long as he thought I could, I was in danger. The problem was that the killer had a way of finding me. He killed my protective detail to get to me at the hotel where they were keeping me. That's when I left town. I figured I couldn't do any worse on my own than with the police, and I wouldn't put any more officers in harm's way. I never stayed anywhere longer than a couple of months because I was afraid he'd get to me. Then one day, I was on a bus heading to Atlanta, and we broke down in Ivy Springs. It wasn't a regular stop, and when I tried to find it on the Internet to learn more about it, nothing came up."

"So you stayed."

She nodded. "I stayed. I only planned to for a few months, but Wally convinced me to stay longer. He gave me a job, paid me in cash, and found me the apartment with Ms. Miller. I paid the rent in cash. We found someone to make me a fake ID. If anyone suspicious came to town, the gossip mill would alert us, and I would stay out of sight. I don't socialize with enough people for anyone to know me or recognize me. I even changed my appearance."

Ben regarded her skeptically. "How? No offense, but you were always blond and blue-eyed."

For a second, she'd forgotten how little he knew about her as an adult. "Oh, um, when I started my own business, I realized very few people took me seriously as a young blond woman. I dyed my hair red, and you would be amazed at how that changed people's attitudes toward me. So when all of that happened with Mr. Warner, everyone knew me with red hair. When I went on the run, I dyed it jet black. After coming to Ivy Springs, Mona helped me get back to my natural color. I never expected to stay here for this long, but when the months passed by without incident, I started to believe I was safe."

"Maybe you are. Maybe whoever was after you is no longer worried that you'll talk."

For a moment, hope sprouted in her chest, and she smiled weakly. "I wish I could believe you're right, but you're not. Since I disappeared, the police somehow uncovered evidence that makes me a person of interest in Mr. Warner's murder. If I turn myself in, I'll be arrested and killed while in custody. I believe that. And there's one more thing that I haven't told you that isn't something your brother would have uncovered."

Ben's eyes narrowed. "You remember."

She nodded, not surprised that he'd guessed. "I remembered who the killer is. As long as I'm around and can testify against him, he has a lot to lose. The minute he can get to me, he'll follow through with what he promised. I believe he'll rape, torture, and eventually kill me."

"Tell me."

Paige wasn't sure she could say the name. She'd kept it to herself for so long, part of her feared that uttering it aloud would bring the devil to her doorstep.

"I saw him on the news several months ago, and it all came back to me as clear as the picture on the TV. Darius Boyd is the man I saw kill Marty Warner."

"Darius Boyd? As in the owner and CEO of DB Network Solutions?"

"One of the richest men in the country," she added . "Yep, that's him."

"Damn, Paige. Are you sure?"

She nodded. "When I saw him on TV, he was standing next to his son, Cassius, as his son announced his intention to run for president of the United States. The camera zoomed in on him, and it was like time stood still for me. I remembered stepping up to the French doors at Mr. Warner's house, and Darius Boyd moved into view with his gun drawn. My mind didn't even register who I was seeing before he pulled the trigger. But when I saw him again, I remembered everything about him. He wasn't wearing a suit like he usually does when he's interviewed or photographed. He had on jeans and a green work shirt. His face was so cold, like it was made of stone. I think he's the one who came after me at the studio and probably at my house."

"I thought you said you didn't see who attacked you?"

"No, but I heard him. When he broke my wrist and told me what he'd do to me. I'll never forget his voice, so when he spoke at his son's press conference, I knew it was him. I can't be sure he was the one who broke into my house and shot the detective or the one who killed my protective detail. But the other times? It was Darius Boyd, no doubt."

"And you've told no one about this?"

"Wally and Mona know I'm hiding from someone dangerous. Ms. Miller has an inkling that I'm in some sort of trouble, but nothing more. And that's it. No one else except for you."

When he didn't say anything more, she wondered if she'd rendered him speechless. She understood that. It was an incredible story, one that rivaled the suspense movie she watched the other night. If she hadn't lived it, she wouldn't believe it.

Paige walked over and sat in a chair next to the couch.

"It's okay. I appreciate your offer to help, but now that I've told you everything, you know how much trouble I'm in. You have a family and a lot more to risk than I do. I'm not mad if you decide to walk away from this. I would if I could."

He enveloped her hand in his. She hadn't realized how cold she'd felt until the warmth from his hands stung her skin.

"I'm not walking away. You can't face this alone. Not anymore. I'm here for you, but you need more help than I can give you by myself."

She shook her head vehemently. "I'm not going to the police, Ben."

"No, not the police. But I need to loop in some other people who can help us. My brothers, to name a few. Some friends of ours who have helped us before."

She stood and tried to pull free, but he only tightened his grasp. "No. I can't, Ben. The more people who know, the more likely it is that I'll be found. I can't do it."

Ben stood too, and his hands gripped her upper arms. "I need you to trust me, Paige. I will never let anything happen to you. *Never*."

"Don't, Ben. Don't make me a promise you have no way of keeping." Her voice was barely above a whisper.

Ben cupped her face with his palm. "I haven't. If you'll trust me enough to bring in my brothers and our friends, I swear to you, we can keep that promise. I can see it in your eyes, Paige. You're tired of running. You're tired of being afraid. Let me protect you. Like you protected me when we were kids."

"The situations are hardly the same."

"No, but we're not the same either. And I'll be damned if I give up a chance to get to know the woman you are now. No one should have to live the way you've been living. All I need is for you to say yes. Say yes, and you have the protection of the Legends."

She barked out a humorless laugh. "Why does this feel like a bad scene in a superhero comic book?"

"Paige," he breathed, his thumb caressing her cheek. "Say you trust me. Say you'll let me help."

She closed her eyes, and she felt his forehead rest against hers. His breath tickled her skin. His presence felt right and made her feel safe.

"Yes." She opened her eyes. "I'm tired of all of it. I trust you to help me. Whatever we have to do, I just want it to be over. I want my life back."

His arms folded around her, and she wrapped hers around his middle. He was all muscle, solid, strong. He made leaning on him easy, and being in his arms was too tempting for her to pull away.

Please. Please don't let trusting him be a mistake.

CHAPTER SEVENTEEN

Paige swung the strap of her overnight bag onto her shoulder. Her eyes swept the studio apartment, nostalgia hitting her like a punch to the gut. She hadn't packed all her belongings, so it's not like leaving meant she'd never see her tiny refuge again. But she knew, regardless of what happened, once she stepped out the door, she wouldn't return to live here.

On impulse, she grabbed the framed photo of her and her parents off the shelf. Ben told her to only take what she needed for a few days, so she hadn't thought to pack it. But she couldn't leave it behind. Wherever she ended up, even if it was temporary, she wanted that piece of her past with her. She needed the reminder of when things were good in her life, when happiness didn't seem out of reach.

Carefully placing the frame in her bag, cushioning it among her clothes so it wouldn't get damaged, she hurried down the stairs and crossed the yard to where Ben waited for her beside his Tahoe, her eyes fixed on the ground in front of her. Eventually, she glanced up, and her steps slowed.

Ben leaned against the front of his SUV. Standing with him were Birdie Miller, Mona, and Wally. Paige hadn't expected them to be there, so she wasn't prepared for the rush of emotions that assailed her. She owed these people quite a bit, and she had no possible way to repay them for their kindness and protection.

Ben stepped up to take her bag and give her an understanding smile. Mona approached her and enveloped her in a tight hug.

"I know what you're thinking, and you're wrong. This is not good-bye. Friends like us never say goodbye. I fully expect you to come back for a visit. We'll enjoy my famous pot roast and caramel cake while we catch up on the incredible life you're living. I believe this will happen, and I insist you believe as well."

Paige pulled back. "Thank you, Mona. For everything. You're the best."

She grinned. "You're right about that," she teased. "Take care of yourself, Char— I mean, Paige. That's going to take some getting used to, but I like it. It suits you."

"You can call me Charlotte if you want. I still like that name. Who knows? Once this mess is over, I might change it for good."

Mona shook her head. "I wouldn't do that. Not when your man there is so fond of your original name."

Paige's eyes flickered over Mona's shoulder to see Ben watching . "He's not my man."

Mona giggled. "Try telling him that. He cares about you. It's written all over him. I'm glad you have him to help, but if he does anything to hurt you, let me know. I don't care how big he is. I'll take him out."

That brought a smile to Paige's lips. "You're a force to be reckoned with, Mona. You take care of yourself and keep your man in line for me."

"Hey, now," Wally interjected. "I heard that. It's not me who needs to behave. This one likes to keep me on my toes.

He planted a kiss to Mona's temple, and the woman's smile widened.

"I'm sorry to be leaving you with only Betsy to clean the motel," Paige told him.

"*Pfffttt*. Betsy, I can deal with. Not having your coffee is going to be hard. That and your company. You're part of the reason I enjoy going to work every day."

She hugged him and kissed his weathered cheek. "I love you. I owe you more than I could ever repay."

Wally shook his head. "It's what friends do. No need to repay anything. Stay safe. And if you need anything, you know who to call."

"Yes, I do."

She approached Ms. Miller, who waited patiently off to the side. Paige didn't speak as she hugged the older woman lightly.

"Thank you for taking me in."

Birdie lifted her shoulder nonchalantly. "It worked out well. We needed each other. Listen, I'm not one for teary goodbyes, so let's skip that part, all right?"

"Deal. See you around, Ms. Miller. You take care of yourself."

"Don't you think it's about time to call me Birdie? And I'm not the one in trouble. You're the one who needs to watch her back."

Paige tilted her head to study Birdie thoughtfully. "How much have you figured out?"

"Enough to know that boy you've hooked up with…He's a good egg, as they used to say. He can help, so let him."

"How can you know that? I barely know him. And I don't think you know what *hooked up* means."

Birdie smirked. "You'd be surprised at what I know. Go, sweet girl. Take care of your business, and when it's safe, you come back, and we'll talk about everything. Sound good?"

"It's a plan."

A few more hugs and waves were exchanged before Ben and Paige drove away.

"You okay?" he asked her.

"No, but I will be. It's just…they're my friends. They were there for me when I felt alone and lost. They knew I was hiding something, but they never asked me to talk about it if I didn't want to. I always thought of this town as my refuge, but it was them. They were my safe haven. I didn't realize it until now."

Ben reached across and grasped her hand, bringing it to rest on his thigh. "You'll be back. You'll see them again. I promise."

Paige tore her gaze away from the passing scenery and stared at his profile. "You like making promises, don't you?"

"Only when I can follow through." He winked at her before turning his attention back to the road.

He kept her hand on his thigh as he drove, and she settled against the seat. Their conversation lulled, so she set his satellite radio to play music. Soon, the stress of the last few days, coupled with the familiar songs, soothed her enough to fall asleep.

Ben opened the door to his house and motioned for her to step inside. The dark interior soon flooded with light. Paige glanced around, studying the space for insight into the man at her back. Ben secured the door and stepped around her.

She thought his expression was anxious, as if he was concerned with her opinion of his home. He needn't have worried. It was what she'd come to expect of the man himself — comforting, safe, no-nonsense. With a woman's touch, it would be perfect.

Paige tucked the thought away, unsure where it came from.

Ben looked around his place as if picturing it through her eyes. "It's not much, but it works for me. Make yourself at home. I'll just put your bag in the guest room down the hall, and then I'll fix us something for dinner."

An unusual trill came from somewhere in the house, and her face scrunched in bewilderment as she tried to figure out where it came from. She heard it again a moment before a furry beast came running into the living room. It skidded to a stop, and through the tufts of hair, golden eyes peered at her.

"That's Ziggy," Ben explained. "Don't mind him. He's not used to company, but he'll adjust. I'll be right back."

He rounded the corner, and she heard his boots thudding against the floor as he moved down the hall. Ziggy stared at her a moment more before racing after Ben, its distinctive trill echoing through the quiet house. Puffs of gray fur hung in the air before wafting down to the floor.

Being in Ben's house left her disconcerted. Taking a page out of his book, she wandered over to a few framed photos he had on the wall. The frames were made of black wood, the photos nothing more than snapshots. One was of four young boys, and she instantly picked Ben out. He was smaller than the others and obviously a bit younger. Their clothes were mismatched and covered in filth. Mud streaked their cheeks, but their shit-eating grins split their faces. Their arms draped over each other's shoulders. Ben and his brothers. She was sure of it.

Another picture was of an adult Ben dressed in fatigues and standing with a man she recognized as his guardian, English Barlowe. The shot was overexposed, so the background was too bright for her to recognize where the photo was taken.

The last one was one she'd never seen before, but she remembered the day it was taken. The elementary school had a harvest festival fundraiser. Each class sponsored a booth, and the event was open to the community. The festival was full of games, prizes, baked goods, arts and crafts, and entertainment. Paige had talked Ben into going with her and her parents. When they thought she wasn't looking, her father had given Ben money to enjoy some of the activities, and she remembered having a blast with Ben at her side.

The festival had a game called a cake walk, and Paige remembered their teacher explaining how the game was played. All she needed to know was that it was like musical chairs, and the winner won the homemade cake that was offered. When the double chocolate fudge cake came up as the next prize, she and Ben decided to compete for it. They were certain one of them would win, and they fell over themselves trying to beat each other.

Ben had won the cake, but then he presented it to her. She insisted it was his, but he told her he didn't want it. He only wanted to have fun with her. Their teacher said the gesture was so sweet, she wanted to take their picture. She captured the image of the two six-year-olds, with their rumpled clothes, messy hair, and crooked grins, holding the sugary dessert between them like it was gold instead of cake.

"I had the best time that day."

She jerked, her hand flying to her chest. "Where did you come from? I didn't hear you come back."

Ben grinned. "It happens. Becky says sometimes I sound like a herd of elephants charging through, and sometimes my footsteps are quieter than church on communion Sunday, whatever that means."

Paige chuckled. "I've never heard that phrase before, but it fits. I'm wondering where you got this picture."

"I stole it."

She gaped at him. "Ben, are you serious?"

"Yep," he said, looking very pleased with himself. "I saw it on the teacher's desk with a bunch of other pictures she took at the Harvest Festival. When no one was looking, I took it and hid it in my notebook. The edges are kind of bent because it came with me to basic training and deployment when I was in the Army."

Her eyes widened. "Really? I, uh, I don't know what to say to that. I just never…Well, I guess I'm surprised…"

His finger touched her lips, effectively silencing her. "I never forgot you, Paige. Outside of my brothers, you were the best friend I ever had."

She lightly grabbed his hand and lowered his finger. Then, rising on her tiptoes, she touched her lips to the corner of Ben's mouth. The roughness of his five o'clock shadow caused her skin to tingle in the most delicious way.

"I feel the same about you."

Her voice was soft, and she was acutely aware of how close their bodies were. She released his hand and placed hers on his chest. His heart thudded underneath her palm. Ben tangled his fingers in her hair, drawing them through the strands slowly, sensually. A shudder wound through her body.

"I'm glad." His voice was deep and low, causing heat to flood her belly. "But I'm no longer interested in being your friend."

His head lowered, his lips hovering over her mouth. If she wanted to stop him, he gave her every chance to do so. But she didn't. She would bet good money she wanted this kiss more than he did.

His lips touched hers, and her mouth opened in response. His tongue dipped inside, tasting her. He pulled her flush against him. Her hands wrapped around his neck to steady herself. Her knees weakened, and she was grateful for his hold keeping her upright. A haze clouded her mind, her senses attuned to his taste, his touch, and the feel of him. Fireworks exploded behind her eyes when he deepened the kiss. Her lungs tightened, begging for air, but she wasn't about to pull away. Desire swept her in a dizzying web, holding her prisoner to the passion lacing the kiss.

Ben was the first to break away. They stared at each other, panting and pulling in deep breaths. His eyes had darkened to almost black, and she was captivated by the fathomless depths. Her fingers tangled in his hair, her eyes memorizing every slope and plane of his face. All traces of the boy she once knew were gone. Left in their place was the evidence of a man who was strong, battle-hardened, and weathered by the tests of time. The result was potent, the substance of every fantasy she'd ever had…only better.

"If friendship's not what interests you," she began, her voice breathy. "What do you want?"

He pressed his forehead against hers. "You, sweetheart."

"And if I tell you that you can have me?"

"Don't say it unless you mean that I can have all of you. I want to explore every inch of your body. I want your heart and your soul to belong to me. I've never had much to call my own, and I've never cared. But you, sweetheart? You were always meant to be mine."

"I want that too. I don't want to focus on the fear or my problems or anything but you. I don't want to feel anything but you, Ben. I want you to touch me, to kiss me, to make love to me, until I forget everything else."

He kissed her again, hard and unforgiving. She tried to push her body closer to his, craving the feel of him, but they were already as close as two people could be. Lowering back to the pads of her feet, she released her hold on him without breaking the kiss. Her hands glided up his torso under his shirt, and she groaned at how smooth and solid his abdomen felt.

With his hands wrapped around her biceps, he gently set her back until the kiss broke. He backed up several steps, and she saw his internal struggle to collect himself. Something she definitely didn't want to happen.

"Why did you stop?" She ignored her whiny tone.

"We can't . Not like this." His voice sounded ravaged, and Paige felt a surge of pride that she had affected him that way.

"I want this, Ben. More than I've wanted anything in a long while."

He shook his head, and she couldn't tell if he was doing it to respond to her or to clear his mind. "Not true. You want your freedom. You want to live without fear. I want that for you, too, but I won't be a distraction to help you forget. When I make love to you, it'll be because we've started something we don't want to end. Not because we're trying to avoid reality."

Her breath hitched when she realized he was right. She did want him. He was good and kind and smart and hot as hell. She had no doubt sex with Ben would ruin her to anyone else. But in the moment, she was using him. He had the power to make her forget anything but him and how he made her feel.

Before she apologized, he dropped a lingering kiss on top of her hair and strode toward the kitchen.

"I'll see to dinner. Make yourself comfortable. Ziggy will keep you company until it's ready."

She hadn't even noticed the animal's return until she collapsed in a chair, stunned by what just happened. Ziggy jumped onto her lap, his fur tickling her face. His long body reached across her lap, and she scooted as far back in the chair as she could to give him room. The cat circled her lap, careful not to slip off. Then he dropped to a heap on her thighs, his head resting on the arm of the chair. A loud rumble erupted from him.

With tentative movements, she stroked his fur, the texture calming her. With each pass of her hand, hair swirled up from his body to float on the air and settle on the floor, on the chair, on her. His warmth and weight relaxed her, and when he gave a low throaty groan as his eyes closed in sleep, she smiled.

She didn't expect Ben to be a cat person, but if a strong and intimidating man like him was going to own a feline, it would be one the size of a small jungle cat. She would have to ask him how he came to own the unusual kitty.

In fact, there was a lot she wanted to ask him. She wanted to know him. He had been right to imply there was too much between them to pursue anything serious right now. She had to resolve the threat on her life before that could happen. But what frightened her almost as much as being hunted by a killer was not being able to put an end to it.

If she didn't stop the threat, she'd have to go on the run again. Ben couldn't give up his life and his work to follow her, to live under a secret persona, never knowing what day would be the one when it all would end for good. She would be on her own again because it would be too dangerous to return to Ivy Springs and bring trouble to the people she loved there.

She heard Ben moving around in the kitchen and the occasional clang of pots and utensils colliding. Ziggy was sound asleep in her lap, and she continued to stroke him. She allowed her thoughts to drift away, to dream of a life that could be if the demons in this one were slain.

CHAPTER EIGHTEEN

Paige gasped as she jolted up in bed. Her heart slammed against her chest, and a light sheen of sweat coated her skin. Her covers were in a tangle around her legs as if she'd been tossing and turning for a while. She gazed around the dark room, trying to remember why she was in the unfamiliar space. When memories of Ben flooded her mind, she relaxed.

Untangling herself, she climbed from the mattress and visited the bathroom. She didn't think she could fall asleep again so soon after her nightmare. Careful not to make too much noise, she slowly opened the bedroom door and crept into the hallway. She turned toward the kitchen to get a glass of water and then skidded to a stop.

Oh, my! The thought flitted across her mind unbidden, but it was apt for the moment.

Ben stood in the open doorway to his room, leaning against the door jamb as if he had all the time in the world. He wore loose sweatpants and nothing else. Her eyes traveled the length of his body. From his bare, well-muscled chest, with only a hint of dark hair along his sternum, to his bare feet, she was entranced by him.

"Paige? Everything okay?"

"Hmmm?" she asked, bemused. "Oh, um, bad dream. I was just going for a glass of water."

He straightened and approached her. Concern darkened his eyes, and when he was in front of her, he placed his fingers under her chin to lift it. His gentle touch sent butterflies fluttering across her stomach.

"Nightmare about Boyd?"

She shrugged. "Probably. I never remember them."

He released her. "You've had them before?"

She nodded. "Since that day at Mr. Warner's house. I never re-member the details. I just wake up frightened. It usually takes me some time to shake it off."

He pulled her into his embrace, and she allowed herself to relax against him. Her head rested on his chest, his heart beating in her ear. The sound was comforting.

"I'm sorry," she said softly, enjoying the feel of his arms around her.

"For what?"

"For earlier. For trying to use you to forget. I didn't realize I was doing it at first. You don't deserve that."

"And what do I deserve?"

She pulled back and searched his face. The man before her was strong and handsome, but there was a hint of the insecure and sad little boy she once knew. She loved that little boy, and she hated to think of him being unhappy for even a moment.

"You're incredible. You deserve only the best things in life."

His finger traced a line down her cheek, and she shivered. "I'm not incredible. I'm human. There's good, and there's bad. There was a time when I didn't care to be used by a woman because I was probably using her too."

"Why are you telling me this?"

"Because you are not like any woman I've ever known. I play pretend when I'm working, but I'm not pretending with you. I'm not using you. I want to get to know you. "

"I want that too."

Their gazes held, and then Ben lowered his head. His tongue teased the seam of her lips until her mouth opened. Then his tongue swirled inside, tangling with hers and tasting the crevices of her mouth. She moaned and clung to him, passion burning within her and spreading throughout her body with the speed of a forest fire. His lips were firm but gentle. Paige moaned as he deepened the kiss, his hand caressing her back as he held her flush against him. Her fingers swirled in the curly strands of his hair, the texture soft.

"Ben," she breathed against his mouth, his rich, woodsy scent enveloping her .

"Paige, I…" His voice trailed away as he kissed a trail down her cheek to her throat. His hand pulled at the neckline of her sleep shirt, so his lips could trace the curve of her shoulder.

"Hmm," she purred. "That feels amazing."

He retraced the path until his mouth paused over the pulse in her neck. "You feel and taste amazing."

He kissed her again as a hand slipped underneath her shirt. His hand slid from her waist to her rib cage, the gentle touch raising goosebumps on her skin. Then his hand cupped her breast, his palm kneading the tender flesh. His thumb circled the taunt nipple, and need curled in her belly.

Pulling away, he lifted her shirt over her head and tossed it to the floor. Holding her breast, he wrapped his lips around her nipple and began his tender assault. He nipped the sweet flesh, then soothed it with a delicate swipe of his tongue. He sucked on the nub until she moaned and arched her back . He repeated the process with her other nipple, dividing his attention between the two until she was writhing in his arms.

"Ben. Oohhh!"

The sensations building within her were powerful, almost too much to bear, but she wasn't about to tell him to stop. The need to touch him propelled her hands to explore. She ran her fingers along the planes of his abs and chest. When she touched his nipples, she gave them a tweak and smiled at the deep groan rumbling from Ben's throat.

"Ben," she moaned. "Please."

He raised his head to capture her lips in a hard, devastating kiss. "What do you want, baby?" His voice was rough and husky, and her insides melted.

"Make love to me. I want you, Ben."

"Whatever you want, baby."

He lifted her, and she wrapped her legs around his waist. She held tight as he kissed her, moving into his room without breaking the contact. Damn, this man could kiss. He carried her to the edge of his bed and then lowered her to her feet. The feel of her breasts sliding against his chest was delicious torture.

Her hands ran over his broad shoulders, down his chest, over his abdomen, and stopped on his waist. Her fingers dipped under the waistband of his sweatpants. Her tongue swiped across her lips.

"What are you waiting for?" He teased her, but his tone was rough, like he was holding to his control by a thread.

She lowered his pants gradually, his hard cock popping out hard and eager. He stepped out of his pants, and she gripped his cock, licking the tip. She smiled at his groan and enclosed her lips over him, her hand squeezing the base. His skin felt like velvet, and the taste of him tantalized her tongue. Her hands reached around to grip his firm buttocks, squeezing them as she sucked him deep in her throat.

"Nope!"

He stepped back until his cock fell from her mouth. He lifted her to her feet, then swept her in his arms. They shared a steamy kiss, and Paige thought she might combust with need.

"Why did you stop me?" Her lips curved into a pout.

"Because I wouldn't have lasted if you kept that up. And I have something else in mind for our first time."

He placed her gently on the mattress, then took his time drawing her sleep shorts and panties down her legs. He settled between her thighs, his smile hungry.

"Beautiful," he murmured.

When his mouth tasted her core, she writhed in ecstasy. Her hands squeezed fistfuls of the bedspread. His lips latched on to her clit and sucked. Her hips bucked, a moan escaping her lips. He placed an arm over her hips to hold her still as he continued to feast. Waves of exquisite pleasure rolled through her until everything around her faded away, leaving only Ben and all the ways he made her body sing.

When his fingers joined the act, her orgasm built to a frantic height. One then two slipped inside her channel, fingertips curling to find her delicate G spot. She exploded, pure bliss coursing through her as she rode the intensity of her orgasm. Ben's fingers continued to tantalize her while his eyes studied her.

"God, you're breathtaking," he said as she came down from her high, feeling wonderfully drained.

"I would like to say something equally as complimentary, but my brain isn't functioning at the moment." Her breath came in short pants, punctuating her words.

Ben crawled up her body, claiming her lips. She was shocked at how quickly her desire rose within her . Her legs encircled his waist, her arms around his neck. He positioned his cock at her entrance, the tip brushing her clit. Her moan was deep and guttural. Her fingers dug into the skin at his back, sliding down a bit harder than necessary, but the pain mixed with their pleasure seemed to spur him on.

With one satisfying thrust, he entered her. He slowly started to move , and her hips met him thrust for thrust.

"More," she whimpered. "Please, Ben. I need more."

His hips moved faster, his thrusts more intense. He reached between them to rub his thumb on her clit.

"Come for me, baby."

And she did. Her orgasm crashed through her, but still he pounded into her. The friction only fueled her orgasm, drawing it out until she thought the tide of pleasure would kill her. Ben tensed and then roared through his own orgasm. They rode out their ecstasy together. Then he collapsed on top of her, careful to brace the bulk of his weight on his legs and arms.

Their pants were heavy and eliminated the need to speak. She held him, relishing in the warmth of his body next to hers. Being with him was everything she could have hoped for and didn't know she needed. He rested his head against her chest, and her fingers caressed his hair. After several minutes, he stiffened and raised his head.

"Oh, shit. No condom."

Paige felt her eyes widen, stunned she'd forgotten that important detail. "Um, well, I'm on the pill, and there hasn't been anybody in a long time. Like so long, I may actually be a virgin again."

She expected him to laugh or even smile at her lame attempt at humor. Instead, he sobered.

"I'm sorry, Paige. I never want to be careless with you, but I swear to you, I'm clean. ."

She placed a hand against his cheek. "Do you wish we hadn't...?"

"Hell, no, but I never want to take advantage of you or make you uncomfortable in any way. Baby, I'm—"

She raised her head and kissed him briefly.

"What was that for?"

Paige smiled. "It was the only way I could think of to stop you from apologizing again. It's okay, Ben. I know you would never hurt me, and I'm protected. Then we'll both be less careless with protection the next time."

His lips curved in a devilish smile. "Next time?"

"And next time. And the next."

"Do you mind if I rest first? The last time threw me for a loop."

He rolled to lay on the mattress and pulled her on top of him. He reached for a blanket at the bottom of his bed and pulled it over them.

Her smile radiated contentment. "It was pretty amazing."

"The timing could have been better with all you have going on."

She shook her head. "It was perfect. Whatever happens with my situation…it changes nothing with us. I won't allow it."

"That makes two of us. Rest, baby. We have a big day tomorrow, and I want to make love to you twice more before then."

She placed her head on his chest and closed her eyes. "Just twice? You disappoint me, Ben Weston. I thought a Legend would be up for so much more."

"Oh, I am, baby. More than you know."

CHAPTER NINETEEN

Paige's eyes appeared too wide and deep gray against her ashen face. Ben wanted to hold her, but he settled for holding her hand. The simple touch was enough to stir his desire, but he tapped it down. His attraction wasn't as important as demonstrating he was there for her.

Seeing the room through her eyes, he understood how overwhelmed she must feel. When the Legends and Atlas worked a case, everyone talked over everyone else, and people volunteered at random to run down leads. It was hard to keep up with who was whom when so much was happening all at once, especially for someone not used to their dynamic.

They congregated in Jackson's house around his dining room table even though it wasn't large enough to accommodate them all. His brothers were there along with Reagan and English. Their group included men from Atlas Security — Jackson's Army buddy and the company's owner Alex Crandell, Turner Drake, who preferred to be called by his last name, PJ Kline, who rarely told anyone what the initials stood for, and two others Ben had never worked with before, Remi Corteman, a woman as unique as her name, and Ridge Henley, who communicated through grunts and nods more than words.

"Paige, I know this is hard, but I think it would be best to start from the beginning. Would you share your story with everyone? " Reagan urged her.

Paige squeezed his hand tightly. He leaned over to whisper in her ear.

"You don't have to. I can tell them, and you can listen or excuse yourself. No one is going to make you do anything you've not comfortable with."

"It's okay," she whispered back, and his chest swelled with pride.

His Paige was strong. As much as he wanted to protect her, she didn't need him for that. She needed his support, and he'd give her that for as long as she wanted it.

She launched into the story, and no one interrupted her. Ben suspected if they did, she wouldn't be able to get through it without losing her composure. When she finished, she leaned against him, and he squeezed her hand again.

Alex moved his hands to speak in American Sign Language. His employees were well versed in ASL, a requirement of their employ, but the only one in his family who understood him was Jackson. After having his larynx damaged, Alex was unable to speak above a whisper, and his voice weakened the more he used it. ASL was his way to communicate, and his employees translated for clients who didn't know how to sign.

"Thank you," Paige said quietly, and Ben turned to her, surprised. "You understand sign language?"

She shrugged. "A little. He thanked me for sharing my story, and he apologized for what I'd been through. You didn't tell me he was deaf or hard of hearing."

"I'm not," Alex signed. "My voice box is damaged, so I don't talk very much. I hear fine, and I can read lips."

At her confused expression, Drake interpreted, and she thanked him with a smile.

"Like I said, I only know a little sign language. Not enough to carry on a conversation, but I'll do my best to follow," she said sheepishly.

Alex's hands moved. "No need. Drake will interpret."

Drake was already speaking each word his boss signed and picked up the narrative at Alex's urging. "And now he wants me to talk about the Warner murder. After Jackson called, I gathered all the facts available on the case. Most of it came from the police file, but there was some other intel that came from more thorough research. Marty Warner was shot as you said. He received rounds from a nine-millimeter semiautomatic pistol. Two in the chest and one at his temple. The second shot was the kill shot, tearing through his lung and ricocheting straight to his heart."

Paige's pallor paled even more, and Ben let go of her hand to place his arm around her. There wasn't much he could do to comfort her, but she smiled at him as if she appreciated his gesture.

"So the shot to the temple was overkill?" English asked.

Drake shrugged. "Either that or the killer wanted to make sure he was dead. Warner's family was also shot. His wife, Delores, took one to the head, execution style. His son, JJ, was shot in the back. His death wasn't instantaneous, according to the medical examiner's report, but he was dead by the time authorities arrived on the scene. His daughter, Francesca, was shot in the chest and bled out before paramedics got there."

Drake paused to take a breath and then continued. "The brass had been policed, and the only clear prints at the scene belonged to family, staff, and Paige. Her camera equipment and cell phone were found at the scene. There were no signs of a struggle and no evidence of theft. Warner was killed first followed by his wife and daughter and then his son. Investigators interviewed the staff and neighbors, but no one could shed any light on the murder. No one saw anything or heard anything. The security cameras were disabled."

"Why shoot the family but not the staff?" Jackson asked.

Drake checked the notes he kept on his secure phone. "According to the report, no staff were working that day. The family was home alone."

Paige sat up straighter. "That's not true. Well, not exactly. There was a maid working in the house, but when I was taking Ms. Warner's portrait, the maid came in to say she needed to go to the grocery store and wanted to know if Ms. Warner needed anything. She was probably still gone when it happened, but she was working. And there were a couple of guys at the stables. One of them took my horse from me when I got back from my ride. The other was cleaning out the stalls."

Drake glanced over his shoulder at Ridge, who was leaning against the wall, quietly listening. "Think you can run down that lead? Find out why there's a discrepancy with the report?"

Ridge nodded and stepped from the room. Ben wasn't sure where he went, but he didn't care. Alex's operatives were good at what they did. Though private security was their bread and butter, running an investigation was second nature to them. They had come through on several cases when the Legends needed their help, and they were considered part of the family.

"After reading the report and talking to one of the investigators, I thought they were thorough in their investigation. Now I'm wondering what more they missed," Drake said.

"Do they have a theory?" Reagan asked.

"They have several, but nothing that fits. They ruled out burglary and robbery. They checked into known associates, but anyone who stood out as a possible suspect had an alibi. Now we know why, since Paige saw Darius Boyd shoot him. He wasn't mentioned in the file as a suspect, but once we had a name to go on, we checked some more," Drake said.

"Warner contributed to Cassius Boyd's election campaign. Delores Warner hosted a fundraiser for Cassius at the country club," PJ explained. "There's your connection, but it's not exactly a motive for murder."

"Is Cassius involved? Maybe he had a beef with Warner and talked his dad into taking him out," Easton said.

"Anything's possible," Alex signed.

"I checked into Warner," Luke said. "His company was profitable, and his financials didn't show anything suspicious. He came by his wealth honestly, but his wife had her own fortune too. They signed a prenuptial agreement when they married that protected both their assets. They had college funds set up for their children, and upon graduation with a degree, the kids each receive trust funds in addition to their college funds."

"Who gets the money now that the family has been killed?" Jackson asked.

"It goes in probate, and what's not used to cover funeral expenses and outstanding debt will go to charity," Luke explained.

"Something's not adding up," English muttered, and Ben agreed.

"I think it comes back to motive. Why would Boyd want to kill Warner?"

"I go back to Cassius. It wouldn't surprise me if he's connected to this somehow," Luke said.

"We can check him out, but honestly, I don't think Cassius is involved."

All eyes turned toward Remi. She stood tall under the scrutiny, but Ben wondered if her assessment was more personal than professional .

"What makes you say so?" Ben asked her.

"I know Cassius. He used to be involved with a friend of mine. Cass is not a killer, nor would he have anyone killed. I'm not even sure he has the stones to survive a career in politics. His father, on the other hand, is a mean son of a bitch. If we can take him down for this, I'd owe you all. Big time."

"It's okay. Tell them," Alex signed.

"Right," she said on a sigh. "The boss wants me to explain my connection to this case. Cass was engaged to my best friend, but his father didn't approve of her. He offered to pay her one million dollars to walk away from Cass and never tell him why. She told him to shove his money up his ass."

Remi smiled as if amused by the memory. "You just had to know Tessa. She spoke her mind and never pulled any punches. She was exactly the type of person Darius deemed unworthy of his son."

"Was?" Paige asked softly.

Remi frowned. "She was killed in a car crash. It was ruled an accident, but I don't think it was. The problem is that her car burned up with her body inside. There was nothing to conclusively rule it foul play. Boyd barely gave Cass time to mourn before he started grooming his son for his political career. Everything about Cass' life has been orchestrated by his father."

"I'm sorry about your friend," Paige responded, and Ben hugged her tightly.

"So I have a question," Reagan changed the subject. "Is it possible that Mrs. Warner and Boyd were involved? They had an affair. Maybe she ended it to save her family. He got mad and decided if he couldn't have her, no one would."

"No," Paige spoke up. "I spent time with them. I took their photos. Mr. and Mrs. Warner both shared with me how they met and how happy they were. Their children joked that it was gross how much their parents doted on each other. I can't see her having an affair and jeopardizing her marriage that way."

"It wouldn't be the first time," English said.

"We might as well check into it even if it doesn't get us anywhere," PJ said. "We have nothing solid to go on, so it doesn't hurt to cover all the bases."

"What charity did you say gets Warner's estate?" Drake suddenly asked.

"I didn't," Luke said. "But there's three. American Cancer Society."

"His mother died of cancer, so that tracks," Drake interrupted.

"The Academic Achievement Society for Excellence," Luke continued.

"They award scholarships to economically disadvantaged students to use for college. Warner was a scholarship recipient at one time, and once he became successful, he started donating to them on a regular basis," Drake explained.

Luke scowled. "Sounds made up to me. Anyway, the third one is the Cartwright Foundation."

"Bingo!" Drake settled back against his chair with a shit-eating grin. "That's the charity run by none other than Nyla Cartwright Boyd. Cassius's wife."

"Another connection to Warner and Boyd," Jackson murmured.

"So we have leads to figure out motive, but we need evidence to tie Boyd to the murder. Otherwise, he'll keep coming for Paige," Ben said.

"He may not have to," Drake said. "The police have Paige listed as their top suspect. The evidence is circumstantial, but we've seen criminals convicted on less. At this point, her testimony will be suspect at best."

"What reason would I have to kill him?" Paige protested.

Drake turned sympathetic eyes to her. "At this point, Paige, the reason wouldn't matter when the only evidence they've found at the scene points back to you. Not to mention you disappeared suddenly. That alone makes you look guilty."

"So what now?" she asked, feeling desperation sink like a boulder to the bottom of her stomach.

"Now, we go after Boyd and find the proof we need to take him down," Ben vowed.

"Damn straight," Remi said. "I know you don't know us, Paige, but we're very good at what we do. The last thing any of us want is for someone like Boyd to walk around free. We'll figure this out. All we need is for you to stay hidden until we do."

Paige sucked in her lips and cast a glance at Ben. He noted the fear that was ever present in her eyes, but there was also something else — determination.

"I think I can manage that," she told Remi. "I've had plenty of experience so far."

Her joke earned grins from the people around them, and Ben squeezed her, hoping she knew how proud he was of her for staying calm and brave when her life was on the line.

"Let's get a plan together." Jackson leaned forward to brace his arms on top of the table. "The sooner we take down this guy, the sooner Paige can have her life back."

And the sooner Ben could convince her to spend that life with him.

CHAPTER TWENTY

The grandfather clock chimed noon, and Darius Boyd took a long swig of his bourbon. Polite society would tell him it was too soon to be drinking hard liquor. To that, he would tell polite society to go to hell. The alcohol had no effect on him, and the bourbon kept him focused.

Sunlight beamed through the windows, casting its rays over the pile of correspondence on his desk. Most business was conducted over text and email these days, but he preferred the old way of doing things. Business lunches, hard copy proposals, mailed invitations, cash over bitcoin. It frustrated those who worked with him and for him, but no one dared to challenge him . He made them a lot of money, and he could snatch it all away before they could blink.

They were loyal to him because of their greed. That was their folly. Oh, he understood greed. He'd made a career out of manipulating people because of the love for money. But he knew what was truly important. Power was far better than money. Power could get him anyone and anything.

He wouldn't tolerate a threat to his power. Steal his money, and he exacted revenge. Go after his power, and he went in for the kill.

A sinister grin curled his lips. Ah, the kill. Talk about the ultimate power trip. He lived for the kill. The ecstasy of holding someone's life in your hands. The potent rush of sealing their fate with one word or one action. It was a high like none other.

He craved it like an addict in need of his next fix, but where an addict grew more desperate the longer they went without, Darius had no such urgency. The longer he waited, the more calculated he was. The more he relished the chase…and the capture.

The knock on his office door was expected. He didn't bother ordering the person inside. Instead, he polished off his drink, poured another, and waited for his visitor to come in.

"I have the information you asked for."

Darius sipped his bourbon slowly, relishing the sweet burn down his esophagus. "Tell me."

His man stepped further into the room, adjusting his tailored suit jacket to conceal the weapon at his side. His eyes were as black as his heart — if he had a heart. He was average height and average build with average features. His complexion gave no clue as to his heritage. Neither did his accent. He was a man without a country, known only by the moniker Mars.

"The people asking questions belong to a private security company, Atlas Security."

Darius raised a brow. "Private investigators?"

"Not really. Primarily security for high-profile clients. No one knows why they're asking questions now, but Remington Corteman is on their payroll."

Darius placed his glass on the bar and turned to face Mars. "The bitch doesn't know when to let it go."

"She knows about the girl."

Darius narrowed his eyes, the only sign of his reaction. "You're sure?"

"I'm sure."

Darius sat behind his desk, the mechanism of his plush leather chair creaking as he leaned the seat back. His elbows lay on the armrests, and his fingers steepled in front of his face.

"I know you don't like to talk, Mars, but I'm going to need more words from you."

The man told his employer what he knew. Atlas Security was sending operatives to ask questions about Marty Warner. Remi Corteman was involved. They found the girl in a Podunk town. The girl was caught on camera along with a known associate of Atlas Security who wasn't an employee. The girl left one Podunk town for another.

The only information that mattered to Darius was about the girl. She was still alive. That needed to change.

"I don't think I have to tell you what's at stake, do I, Mars?"

"No, sir."

"We could lose everything if we don't clean this up and soon."

"I'll take care of it," Mars vowed.

"No," Darius said slowly. "I want the girl."

"Sir?"

"The girl belongs to me. Bring her to me. Take care of anything or anyone who stands in your way."

"Anything *and* anyone?" Mars didn't need the clarification as much as he wanted to savor his directive.

"Whatever it takes."

This time, when there was a knock on his office door, Darius responded.

"Just a minute!"

He looked back at Mars, but the man was already slipping out a different exit. Mars had his orders. He would carry them out flawlessly. All Darius had to do was wait. The girl would be his soon enough, and he would show her exactly what a mistake it was for her to run.

"Come in," he finally called.

His son breezed through the door with all the confidence and polish he was bred to have. Dressed in an expensive navy suit accented with a blue tie and matching pocket square, he wore the million-dollar smile that was made perfect by years of orthodontia.

"You're not going to believe this." Cassius Boyd waved a piece of paper in the air as if it were a first prize ribbon from a county fair.

"I don't know about that. If it's good news for you, I'll believe it."

"It's the best possible news. I got a call from Patty Whitfield with MLD Holdings. They are giving me their endorsement. They pledged half a million dollars to start."

Darius flashed a bright smile that he knew would please his son. "Wonderful! We should celebrate. Dinner at Château de Lumière? My treat."

Cassius beamed. "Sounds perfect. I'll tell Nyla. She'll be up for dinner at her favorite French restaurant. Will Mom be able to join us?"

Darius barely suppressed a look of disdain. "Octavia left earlier today for New York. I don't believe she plans to be back until Sunday."

"Then she'll be back for the next speaking engagement?"

Darius dipped his head in a brief nod. "Yes. She won't miss it. We'll both be there. We want to be with you every step that you're on the campaign trail."

"All our plans are coming together, Dad."

This time, Darius' smile was genuine. "That they are, Cass. We're going to have everything we deserve."

CHAPTER TWENTY-ONE

"You all right?"

Paige turned from the window and smiled at Bailee as she came into view with Dylan resting on her hip. She had just changed the little guy's diaper in one of the back bedrooms of Ben's house. Paige had taken advantage of the moment of solitude to study the neighborhood through the front window, careful to stay out of sight of anyone passing by as Ben had instructed her to.

"Honestly, I think I'm going a little stir crazy."

Bailee chuckled as she placed Dylan on the floor where he could play with his toy cars. Ziggy watched the little boy with feigned disinterest from the platform of his scratching post. Bailee curled her legs underneath her as she snuggled deep into the couch cushions.

Paige said in a chair next to her. Ziggy took the opportunity to jump from his perch and crawl into her lap, as had become his habit over the past few days. She'd grown accustomed to him, so her lap never felt right unless the furry monster was snoozing on it.

"I guess this seems like overkill, doesn't it?" Bailee gave her a sympathetic look that Paige loathed to see, even if she did appreciate her new friend's presence.

"No, I understand why I have to lay low."

Alex Crandell broke the news to her the day after she met with everyone. She had been caught in a background shot by one of the news cameras in Ivy Springs. The footage only aired on a local news program, but it was still a public broadcast, one that could have been seen by anyone with cable access or an online subscription service. One that could have been seen by Darius Boyd.

Since then, she'd been confined to Ben's house with Bailee, Reagan, and Melody taking turns staying with her when Ben wasn't home. The others were chasing leads like a dog chasing its tail, and the results, so far, proved just as futile. Her frustration was rivaled only by her boredom.

Bailee regarded her. "It's hard, but you'll be safe as long as you do what we ask of you."

Paige blew a breath out of her mouth, and it stirred the hair falling to her forehead. "I know, and I will. I'm just used to staying busy, and I ran out of things to do yesterday."

"Yeah. I noticed you could eat off the floor, it's so clean in here."

Paige shrugged. "What can I say? I get anxious. I clean. It's what I've done just about every day for the past year."

"I can kind of understand what you're going through. Has Ben told you how Easton and I met?"

"Not really."

Bailee accepted the car her son handed her. When he went back to playing, she started her story. "He lives next to my Gran. I was a police detective in Kentucky, and after I arrested my partner for murder, I needed a break. I came for a visit and tried to busy myself with home improvement projects. Easton offered to help, so he could flirt with me."

Paige chuckled. "I haven't known your husband very long, but that sounds just like him."

Bailee smirked. "Sounds like you've known him long enough. He's a good man, though. They all are."

"I see that."

Bailee tilted her head as if weighing what to say next. "You seem to be settling in here just fine."

Paige raised a brow. "Why do I get the feeling you have a question you want to ask me, but you're not sure you should?"

"Because I do, but it's none of my business."

"I'm guessing it's about Ben."

Bailee nodded. "He cares about you. I can't help but wonder what will happen when this is over, and you're free to live your life as before."

Paige shook her head. "There's no going back to before. I'm a different person now. And I care about Ben, too. I don't know what that means beyond the here and now. I really can't think that far into the future."

"Fair enough," Bailee said. "Has he kept you up to date on the investigation?"

"He has. I'm just ready for it all to be over."

Ziggy raised his head a minute before she heard Ben's key turning in the lock. The cat ran to greet his owner as he stepped through the door. Dylan toddled over to Ben, too, talking to his uncle in the hurried speech of a one-year-old that was a mixture of gibberish and mispronounced words.

"Hey," Bailee greeted as she stood to her feet. "Welcome home. Any news?"

"Nothing new to report today."

Ben swung his nephew into his arms, and Paige's heart melted at the sight. The man had a way with people, especially children, which fascinated her. He certainly knew how to make her feel special. Each day she'd been staying with him was spent visiting with his sisters-in-law and finding ways to keep busy. Each night, she shared a meal with Ben as he told her news on the case, which hadn't been much.

They ended their evening in front of the television, snuggling together on the couch. The snuggling led to kissing and touching, and before they slept, Paige would fall apart in Ben's arms during a sizzling round of sex. Sometimes they would make it to the bedroom. Other times they never made it off the couch.

Though she was still plagued with the occasional nightmare, Paige slept better in Ben's arms than she had in the last year. He made her feel cherished, but more than that, he made her feel safe. It was a feeling she never wanted to take for granted.

Bailee gathered her son and their things in short order. Giving Paige and Ben a hug, she was out the door in record time. Paige stepped into Ben's arms as he drew her close for a searing kiss.

"Damn, I missed you," Ben breathed against her lips, and her stomach did a flip.

"I'm happy to see you, too." Her smile was serene but happy.

He lifted his head, and his eyes searched hers. She wasn't sure what he was hoping to see, but her eyes spoke the words she hadn't said out loud. This man was special to her. If she could come out from under the danger she was in, she wanted to be with him. Moments like this, when she was in his arms, and they exchanged passionate kisses that left them both hot and bothered…well, they were her proof that Ben wanted to be with her, too.

"I love you, Paige."

Her smile froze on her face, and her eyes grew so wide she expected them to pop from the socket. "Ben, I—"

His hand rested lightly on the side of her neck. "My timing sucks. I get it. I just wanted you to know how I feel."

Her brow furrowed. "Is something wrong? Did something happen today?"

His intense expression relaxed. "Shit, no. Sorry. I didn't mean to worry you. I missed you, and having you in my arms, having you here when I get home, it feels right. It's made me realize how much you mean to me."

Her hands framed his face and pulled him in for a sweet kiss that showed him she felt the same way.

"I love you too."

"Paige, I didn't tell you because I expected—"

She placed a finger over his lips to stop him. "I'm telling you because it's true. And tonight, I'll show you it's true."

Ben's nostrils flared, and heat simmered in his eyes. "I like the sound of that."

They kissed again. This time, the kiss was frantic. They devoured each other as if they couldn't get enough. And she was sure she never would.

His hands gripped her hips and then slid up under her shirt to touch the skin of her waist and her stomach. Goosebumps rose in response to his touch, and waves of pleasure rolled over her. She fantasized about this, about him. But reality was... So. Much. Better.

He pulled back and touched his forehead to hers, as was becoming his habit. She loved how he seemed to always want to touch her. He held her hand, or draped an arm over her shoulders, or touched foreheads. The attention made her feel special and wanted.

"Oh, baby, I want to take you into that bedroom and strip off your clothes until you're standing in front of me like the naked goddess you are."

She smiled wickedly. "Sounds perfect to me."

"In due time, sweetheart. The first order of business though is a shower and dinner . We're going to need our strength for the night I have planned."

She laughed. "I guess I can live with that. Go. Grab your shower. I'll start dinner, and then our evening together can begin."

He dropped another kiss to her lips. "I can update you on your case over dinner."

"I thought you said there was nothing new."

He shrugged. "There's not really. But I want you to be kept in the loop every step of the way. It's not fair to keep you in the dark when your future is on the line."

Paige sighed. "I appreciate that, but let's not talk about the mess I'm in tonight. I just want to focus on us."

"Us. I like the sound of that." His lips spread in a slow, sultry smile. "I'll be quick."

She watched him move toward his bedroom, her eyes drinking in the sight of his broad shoulders, bulging arms, and firm ass. Her mouth watered to think of the night that awaited her. They'd only reconnected a short time ago, but somehow, she felt like she had yearned for Ben her whole life. To hear that he loved her was everything.

Her smile was wide as she went to his kitchen. She searched the cabinets and refrigerator before deciding on what to prepare for dinner. She wasn't much of a cook, but what she did know how to create was pretty good. And tonight's dinner had to be the best she'd ever prepared. She wanted their time together to be perfect.

She placed fettuccine noodles in water to cook and began preparing a creamy sauce when her phone buzzed . She stared at the device, surprised to be getting a call when only a select few had her number. Of those few, Ben was the one who used it often. Turning the heat down on her sauce, she reached for the phone only to see that the call came from an unknown number.

She almost didn't answer. After all, she had a sexy man in the shower who promised her a night to remember. And an unknown member usually meant the call was spam. On impulse, she swiped to accept it before it went to voicemail.

"Hello?"

"Hello, Paige."

The deep voice held no emotion. The tone was even and calm, but Paige recognized it instantly. Her hand shook, and she tightened her grip to keep from dropping her phone.

"H-how did you get this n-number?"

Her heart pounded so loud that she almost didn't hear him over the rush in her ears.

"That's not important. I don't want to waste time talking about subjects that are not important."

She swallowed the lump in her throat. Memories surged to the surface despite all the time that had passed. She closed her eyes to will them away, but she ended up giving them room to play in her mind. He had come from nowhere, grabbing her from behind when she left her photography studio. His glove-encased hand clamped over her mouth hard enough to leave faint bruising on her face. The hold that secured her arms to her body had been strong, like a vise ensnaring her. The voice in her ear threatened to kill her if she made a sound.

Not only had she made a sound, but she damaged his shin trying to escape him.

"What do you want?"

"I think that is obvious, Paige. I want you."

"Forget it, asshole. You can't have me."

He made a sound that could have been a laugh, but there was no humor or joy in the noise.

"When you hear what I have to say, you'll change your mind."

Steam started shooting up from the pasta, and she hurried to turn off the stove eye underneath it and the pan with the pasta sauce.

"Somehow, I doubt that."

Her retort was met with silence, and she checked her screen to make sure the call was still connected.

"Charlotte? You there?"

Her hand snapped the phone back to her ear. "Ms. Miller? Oh my God! Are you—"

"It's a shame," the man continued. "For this old woman to be in danger because of you, and she doesn't even know your real name."

"If you hurt her—"

"Idle threats are cliché, wouldn't you agree? There's only one way for me not to hurt this woman. You come to me. I let her go. It's as simple as that."

Paige's mouth went dry, and her stomach lurched. She closed her eyes to stave off the nausea. "I don't believe you. Instead of letting her go, you'll kill us both."

"But you'll come anyway, won't you, Paige? I'll make this simple for you. Take your boyfriend's SUV. If you leave now and drive straight through, you can be here in four hours and ten minutes. Just in case, I'll give you four hours and fifteen minutes to make it. If you're not here in that time, she's dead."

"Wait! I can't do that. If I take the SUV, he's going to track me down. What if there's an accident on the way? What if I run out of gas on the way? You can't—"

"I hold all the cards, Paige. I can do whatever I want. But I can be a reasonable man. Let's make it four hours and thirty minutes. If you're late, she's dead. If anyone follows you, you're all dead. If you tell anyone where you're going, you're...All...Dead."

The call ended, and Paige felt her heart stop when she realized he never told her where she was going. In the next moment, a text came through with an address in Biloxi, Mississippi, and she almost fainted in relief. A sob escaped her throat, but she ruthlessly pulled herself together. Now wasn't the time for a breakdown.

Her thoughts raced. She no longer heard the shower, which meant Ben would be back any second. *All dead.* The man's words played on repeat, ringing in her ears with a sinister finality she couldn't escape. She shoved her phone in her pocket and ran toward the door. Ziggy trilled behind her as she snatched Ben's keys from the table in the foyer. Her hand landed on the doorknob when she heard Ben behind her.

"What are you doing?"

She didn't turn around. If she did, she'd lose her nerve.

"I have to go."

"I heard. I'm not letting you go alone."

She closed her eyes. "I have to. He'll kill her."

"He'll kill her either way. And you, too. You have to trust me."

She whirled around. "I do. But I don't have a lot of time."

She could see the different emotions warring on his face, and her eyes pleaded with him to understand. Finally, he hardened his expression and dipped his head in a single nod.

"Go. I'll find you. We'll end this."

Paige nodded, tears falling down her cheeks. "I love you, Ben."

She slipped out the door and ran to his Tahoe, giving in to the sobs and the fear of what faced her at the end of the road trip.

CHAPTER TWENTY-TWO

"**T**ake a left."

Jackson jerked the steering wheel without slowing his speed, following the directions Luke supplied. Ben sat in the back seat, trying not to lose his shit. Seated beside him, Easton stared him down. Probably attempting to decide if he was, indeed, going to lose his shit.

"Incoming!" Luke shouted.

Luke tapped a key on his laptop, and the men in the SUV listened. The ringing coming across the speakers sounded garbled. When Paige's voice answered the call, Ben's heart lurched in his chest.

"What?" Paige snapped.

Good girl, Ben thought. She wasn't showing this guy an ounce of fear, though he knew she was full of it. His hands clenched into fists, gripping the fabric of his black cargo pants.

"I would be careful with how you speak to me, Paige. I am the one holding all the cards."

Ben committed the sound of the man's voice to memory. The deep, clear tone measured his words. He was careful not to let emotion seep into his voice. He revealed no more intel than he wanted her to know, but he knew what to say to push Paige's buttons.

Ben was already looking forward to killing the son of a bitch.

"I'm on my way. I'm less than an hour out. What else do you want from me?"

Paige's voice rose in anger and not panic, which gave Ben a

small measure of relief. If she was going to get through this, she needed her wits about her.

"I want you to pull over at the next exit. Turn right, and there is a gas station on the left. Turn into the parking lot, drive around to the back, and leave your vehicle in front of pump number seven. Get out. Leave the keys and your phone behind. Go to the car parked at pump number ten. Get in it. The keys are under the right front floor mat. Drive it the rest of the way here."

Ben frowned. The asshole was taking precautions so Paige couldn't be tracked. The bastard was smart. Calculated. A pro.

"I need my phone for directions. I can't leave it behind," Paige protested.

"There's a phone in the other car. It's preprogrammed with the address I got you."

"You left a car, unlocked, with the keys and a cell phone inside. That wasn't smart," Paige snapped.

"Do not underestimate me."

The call ended.

"Get anything?" Ben asked anxiously.

"No. The signal was pinging all over the place. No way to trace the call," Luke said.

Paige's voice came across the speaker again. "I hope you guys are listening and got all of that. He's forcing me to leave everything behind, so I hope my earrings are working the way you said they would. Because I'm plenty scared."

Ben's eyes closed as he fought the urge to call a stop to all of it.

"Your woman's a brave one."

Ben opened his eyes and met the reflection of Jackson's in the rearview mirror. "We didn't plan on them kidnapping one of her friends."

"No, but our plan will still work. Hang in there, brother."

He didn't respond, and Jackson didn't expect him to. His brothers understood the thin hold he had on his control . But their plan was solid. He had to trust it. He had his brothers and the support from Atlas Security to help him protect Paige. He trusted them with his life, but he had a harder time than he thought in trusting them with the woman he loved.

When they realized Paige had been caught on camera being in Ivy Springs, the Legends started making plans. It wouldn't be hard for Boyd to connect her to Ben if he looked into her time in Ivy Springs, so they wanted to be prepared in case Boyd found her and abducted her. It was impossible to know all the variables they were dealing with, but their plan covered a lot of scenarios.

The small stud earrings she wore were tracking and listening devices. With a simple touch to the front and back simultaneously, she could deactivate the signal, so they couldn't detect the transmitter in the simple jewelry if they used a scanner to check. The only drawback was that while they could hear her perfectly, they couldn't communicate with her. The idea to use the one-way transmitter had been hers. She worried she would react to the voices in her ear, as she referred to them.

In their experience, planning for the unexpected was business as usual, and Ben was glad they knew to plan for multiple contingencies. Especially in situations like this one, where the man was making calls they didn't expect and giving Paige instructions they didn't foresee.

While the directives seemed amateurish, Boyd proved that he was sharper than he seemed. Having her ditch the phone and the Tahoe before she reached the destination would throw Ben and the others off track. Well, it would if they didn't already have the address he sent her.

"Any word from the operatives tailing Boyd?" Jackson asked, pulling Ben out of his musings.

"Alex has Remi and Ridge tailing him, and the last report was Boyd was at his house in Biloxi. But it's not the address Paige has," Easton said.

"And is about an hour away from where Paige is supposed to change vehicles. So he has someone helping him set her up. Any idea who that could be?" Jackson kept his eyes on the road as he theorized.

I've been working with Atlas' tech guy to track down known associates of Boyd's, but no one raised any red flags," Luke responded.

"Got a message from Alex," Easton said after he checked a notification on his phone.

Alex and his operatives from Atlas were able to fly ahead to Biloxi while the Legends trailed Paige by vehicle. The Atlas guys weren't going to breach unless they believed Birdie Miller was in immediate danger. They would wait for Paige and the Legends to arrive, and hopefully they would find Boyd at the destination along with anyone helping him.

"Holy shit!" Easton yelled. "Alex said they're at the location. It's an abandoned lot. There's nothing but dirt. No one's there. It's a bogus address."

"So are they planning another switch when Paige gets there?" Luke asked just as they heard Paige over the transmitter.

"I'm taking the exit now."

Ben listened to the exchange, his mind whirling with theories. Why would Boyd risk a vehicle exchange just to send Paige to a bogus address? Was Boyd calling the shots or was his associate orchestrating the whole thing? What was their end game?

Ben's gut churned, and his blood ran cold. "Jackson, close the distance. Book it. *Now!*"

"What's up?" Easton asked as the SUV sped down the interstate, breaking every traffic law that kept them from reaching Paige.

"The bogus address. The car switch with the new phone. It doesn't make sense. Why risk any of that if he's planning to kill her?"

"He's not planning to kill her," Jackson surmised.

"He told Paige when he attacked her a year ago that he wanted to torture her, not kill her. I think that's still his plan. He just needs her where she's easier to get to. Which means—"

"It's a trap," Jackson said. "He's going to snatch her at the gas station and take her somewhere else.".

"Not him," Easton reminded him. "He's at his house. Whoever's helping him is going to grab her, and none of us know who he is or what he looks like."

Paige's voice sounded again. "I see the car. It's black. I'm not sure of the model. I'm parking. Here goes."

Ben wanted to scream at her to get back in his Tahoe and drive away as fast as she could. His fingers folded over the top of Jackson's seat and dug into the leather.

"What the…Who are you…What are you doing…No! No! I have to go! I have to…"

Paige's voice was replaced with sounds of a struggle. Ben raked his hands through his hair, feeling a mixture of fury and terror flood his body until he had to react or explode.

"Dammit!" He slammed his fists into the back of the driver's seat, the punches coming in quick succession until Easton nudged him.

"Alex and his team are rerouting to our location. But there's something else."

Ben struggled to catch his breath, but his lungs couldn't seem to draw enough air. He wasn't sure he could handle any more news that made him realize just how much danger his Paige was in.

"Paige is moving, but no audible noise coming from the coms," Luke interrupted.

"I'd bet good money that whoever kidnapped her threw her in a trunk and took off. There's the exit. Easton, Luke, you guys question the service station clerk and customers to see who saw anything. Ben, you and I will take the scene for evidence of where he could be taking her. E, what ya got?"

"A message from one of Alex's techs back at Atlas. The call Paige received from her landlady? It was a deepfake. A good one, but with Atlas' technology, they figured out it was AI-generated."

Artificial intelligence? Boyd was going through a lot of trouble to get to Paige, but he wanted her alive.

Jackson skidded to a stop in front of the pump with the abandoned car that was left for Paige. He twisted around in his seat, his expression grave.

"Boyd can't risk being exposed by coming after Paige himself. We already know he's got someone working with him, and the guy is good. None of Boyd's known associates have been flagged as accomplices, so we need to think bigger. Boyd wouldn't trust just anyone, and he would need someone who knew how to fly under the radar. Someone who has no reservations about doing whatever needs to be done to complete the job. We find him, we find Paige."

A calm determination settled over Ben. "Then let's find him. Because I'm getting her back alive. She's it for me, man. I can't lose her."

"She's one of us now. You're not losing her. Whatever it takes, we'll get her back."

Ben knew the magnitude of the vow his brother just made. In situations like this, when things could go wrong in a hurry, they knew better than to make a promise like that. There was no guarantee they would find Paige, and the probability of finding her alive was even less. But the Legends have been known to pull out a miracle when they needed it.

"We've got your six, brother," Easton added. "We've got your girl's back, too."

Ben nodded. "Then let's quit wasting time. Move your asses. We've got an asshole to track."

CHAPTER TWENTY-THREE

"**W**ake up, you little bitch."

Paige fought through the blackness toward the soft, almost friendly voice uttering the vile insult in her ear. Her head felt heavy and ready to explode. The pain almost had her giving in to the darkness once more, just to escape the agony. Her skin was tingling with a sense of danger that she didn't understand. When she tried to shift her position, her limbs wouldn't cooperate. A sharp pain set her shoulder on fire, and she gasped at the sudden throbbing.

Where am I? What happened?

Her mind refused to focus. Her eyes felt too heavy to open, so she took a mental inventory of her situation. Her wrists and ankles were bound, but she was sitting. The surface underneath her was hard and unforgiving. A floor, possibly? A chair?

Her mouth was dry, and her tongue felt fuzzy as if she'd spent the night drinking and woke with the worst hangover she'd ever felt in her life. But she didn't think that's what happened. And who was the guy? The gaps in her memory were wide, and she couldn't concentrate enough to figure out how to bridge them.

"Wake up!" The voice was harsher and was followed by a slap across her cheek.

Paige's gasp caught in her throat, and she coughed violently, moaning at the excruciating pain that wrecked her body.

"Open your eyes, or I'll glue them open. Permanently."

She shuddered, believing he meant what he said. *You can do this*. The inner pep talk fell flat, but she somehow managed to pull her heavy lids open. The man in front of her didn't look familiar and wasn't who she expected. Instead of Darius Boyd, she saw an average-looking man in a custom-made suit with ice in his dark eyes.

"Finally. How are we feeling? Hmmm? No need to answer. I believe I can guess." The man started pacing in front of her, moving in a methodical circle, his shiny black shoes tapping against the dingy hardwood floor. "Your mouth feels dry like it's stuffed with cotton. Your neck feels too weak to support your head, but you need it to, since your head feels like it's being squeezed in a vise. You feel like you could fall asleep and never wake up, but you can't let that happen, can you?"

He stopped. Then his steps took him directly in front of her. To see his face would require lifting her head, which was an impossible feat in her state, so she stared at a button on his suit jacket.

"You're trying to remember where you are and why you are here, but your brain won't cooperate. In fact, you can barely remember your own name. Your wrists and your ankles feel sore and raw. Your eye feels swollen, your cheek smarts, and you feel ready to lose the last meal you ate. How did I do?"

His assessment was spot on, but she couldn't force herself to admit it.

"Well, now that we've settled how you feel, let me enlighten you as to why. You see, we have a mutual friend who has a keen interest in your welfare. That is, he wants to see you suffer as much as possible. He wants you to beg for your life and then beg for your death. He's been trying to find you for a very long time, but you have outsmarted him. And me as well. You should feel proud. There aren't many alive who can outsmart me."

The man paused, stared at her for a long moment, and then resumed his pacing. "No, I don't suppose you can feel much of anything at the moment except pain, confusion, and fear. All justifiable emotions. Right now, you're feeling the effects of the potent drug I gave you. That was to subdue you for the car ride to our location and to keep you compliant while we wait for our…friend."

"Do I…know you?" Paige's voice sounded strange, like it belonged to someone else.

"Yes, we've met before, although some time has passed. The first time was at your home. The second time you were with those imbeciles who were trying to protect you."

"You killed them. You tried to kill me." Her words were slurred and garbled, but she was certain he understood her.

"Yes. You're a more formidable opponent than I gave you credit for. I have to say, I'm sorry to see the chase end. To think, you were holed up in some backwater town all this time. For a stupid little girl, you covered your tracks well. Kudos to you."

Snippets of memory flashed in her mind's eye, but they weren't enough for her to piece together and understand. Trying only made her head hurt more.

"You shouldn't fight the effects of the drug. It will wear off soon enough, and then the fun can begin."

"Who are you?"

His laugh was pure evil, ringing in her ears until she winced.

"My name is not important. Few people know it, and you won't have time to use it."

"I don't…understand." The room was spinning, and spots appeared in front of her eyes.

"You will. When our friend arrives."

"So…tired."

"Yes, I'm sure you are. You should probably get some sleep. That sounds good, don't you think, Paige?"

She was already slipping into the bliss of unconsciousness. She figured the man wouldn't expect an answer anyway. He seemed to already know what she was thinking and feeling without her saying a word. Her head fell forward, and her eyes closed. She drifted into slumber away from the pain and the torment of her situation.

The slap struck her with enough force to whip her head back and jerk her out of sleep. She moaned as her head fell forward, her neck no longer able to hold it up.

"You think I'm going to let you sleep, you little bitch?"

Paige jerked when the man shouted, and a moan slipped from her lips because of the ensuing pain. "Why…why…"

He gripped her chin and wrenched her head up at an unnatural angle. Beady eyes stared down at her in disgust.

"Why am I doing this to you? That's a good question. And you'll have an answer very soon."

She whimpered when he released her. She needed to do something, but she couldn't get her body or her mind to function through the fog she was in. Tears welled in her eyes and spilled onto her cheeks. Since her hands were bound, she couldn't wipe the tears away, so she closed her eyes tightly to stave off the flow.

"I see you need some help staying awake. I happen to have something right here that can help with that."

Something sharp pierced the skin of her bicep through her shirt and drew downward, leaving searing pain in its wake. Paige cried out, using the last of her will to turn her head. The cut was deep, the blood escaping in thick spurts. The man thrust one more time before withdrawing the blade. A gleam lit his eyes, and a smile curled his lips. He was pleased, almost happy, with the injury he inflicted.

Paige felt her resolve strengthen even as her body grew weaker. The man delighted in her pain and was just beginning his long torture of her. She'd unwittingly given him what he wanted, and as impossible as it felt in her diminished state, she couldn't show him how she suffered. She couldn't let him see the depth of her pain.

Of course, that was easier said than done, she thought before she fainted.

"Talk to me, brother."

Ben stayed silent. His brain had shut down to everything but the investigation. It's what he had to do. To open himself up to more meant he would lose his mind. His Paige was in the hands of a murderer who promised to subject her to horrendous things because she happened to be in the wrong place at the wrong time. Despite their best efforts, Ben hadn't protected her the way he promised.

If he allowed himself to contemplate the enormity of how much he let her down, he couldn't function.

"Nothing to say," Ben muttered, hoping Jackson would let the matter drop.

"I need to know where your head is at."

Ben pierced his brother with a hard stare. "You know where my head is at. You've been here before."

With the reminder of the time when Reagan and her mother, Traci, were kidnapped by someone obsessed with Traci, Jackson nodded. "It's not the same situation."

"Did you feel panic? Did you feel helpless? Did you wonder what the point of all those years of training and helping people was when you couldn't help the one person who needs you the most?"

"Yes," Jackson responded honestly.

Ben stood with his arms crossed over his chest, staring at the crime scene as if the missing piece that would lead them to Paige would jump out at him. But nothing about the abandoned car or the gas station or the patrons that came and went revealed anything to him. They had been without contact with Paige for going on an hour. The transmitter in her earrings had gone offline soon after she was abducted, leaving them with no idea of how to continue.

"How did you deal?" Ben's voice caught, and he pressed his lips tightly closed while he tried to get his emotions under control.

"Tell me about her."

Ben glared. "Are you shitting me right now? Now's not the time for a gossip session."

"Fine. Then I'll tell you. She's a coward. It's her own fault that she's in this mess. She's lucky she's made it this long because she's too stupid to know how to avoid trouble. She's weak—"

Ben's fist flew out at lightning speed, connecting with a satisfying crunch to Jackson's jaw. His brother's head jerked to the side, and he backed up a couple of steps from the force of the blow. Ben lunged at him, but Jackson caught his brother in a bear hug, trapping Ben's arms at his side. Then Jackson shoved Ben away, squaring off.

"That's how I dealt. I focused on all the ways Reagan had it in her to survive. That's what you have to do too. Paige is strong, smart, and a complete wild card. She hid from these people for over a year, not an easy task, but she did it. She'll hang on until we find her, and we'll find her because that's what we do. So get your shit together, brother, or you're benched."

"Like hell!" Ben thundered.

"There are three of us and one of you. If I decide to bench you, you'll be benched."

Jackson's phone rang. He turned his back on a seething Ben to take the call.

"Gish."

"Put it on speaker," Ben ordered, struggling to get a hold on his anger.

English's voice came through the phone's speaker.

"I called a buddy of mine. Asked some questions about Boyd. His son is squeaky clean, but Darius is scum. He's on the radar of every alphabet agency our government has, but his hands are clean. My buddy says Darius has a partner who does his dirty work. No one knows who he is or what he looks like. All they have is an alias. Mars."

"Mars? Like the planet?" Jackson rolled his eyes.

"Like the Roman God of War from mythology," Ben muttered.

"Word is the guy is deadly, but he doesn't act without orders. Mars won't make a move on Paige without Darius' directive. Count on it."

"Got it. Thanks, Gish." Jackson started to end the call when English spoke again.

"Ben, you there?"

"Yeah, Gish."

"Hang in there. We'll get her back. They'll pay for this."

"Thanks, Gish."

Easton came running out of the gas station where he was questioning the clerk and checking out the sorry excuse for security footage the station had. Ben stiffened, knowing from his brother's sprint that he had news.

"Hey, Alex texted. Darius is on the move. Remi and Ridge are still tracking him, and he's heading in this direction."

Ben's heart raced. "She's still around here somewhere. She's close by."

Easton nodded. "That's my guess. And I have a description. The guy who took her showed up about fifteen minutes before Paige did. He paid the clerk to shut off the security cameras. The guy thought there was about to be a drug deal, so he took the money and shut down the cameras. Then, to cover his own ass, he noted the guy's description and the plate number on the car the guy was in. The clerk didn't see the abduction or which direction the guy went when he left because he didn't want to be a witness to whatever was going down. Cost me a hundred bucks, but the clerk gave me the intel he wrote down."

"So what now? We get Luke to hack into traffic cams and see if we can track the car?" Ben asked.

Jackson shrugged. "Where we are, I doubt we'll find a lot of traffic cams to help us out."

Easton grinned. "Nope, we have something better. We have Atlas with eyes in the sky. When Alex realized the Mississippi address was bogus, he knew they wouldn't be able to reroute the plane quick enough to be useful to us. So he had PJ and another operative rent a chopper and head this way. Luke is coordinating with them to track the vehicle."

"So we wait," Ben said, trying to tap down his frustration.

Waiting made him feel useless. He wanted to *do* something to find Paige. She was counting on him to follow through, and all he could do was twiddle his thumbs.

"No," Jackson said. "We drive. We came north to this location. There's nothing south of us except for commercial property. He's going to take Paige somewhere hidden, quiet, where they can't be disturbed. I checked out an aerial map. There are possibilities east and west of us, but if it were me, and I had torture in mind, I would head west. It's more rural and isolated. We start in that direction and close in when we narrow down the location."

"Let's move," Easton agreed and jogged over to their vehicle, where Luke was already waiting.

Jackson set out to follow, and Ben nudged him. "Hey, thanks."

Jackson touched his jaw. "Don't thank me yet. You got a pass until we find your girl. Then your ass is mine."

Ben barked out a brief laugh. "You wish."

Jackson cracked a smile. "Let's go get your girl."

"I love her, Jackson. She's it for me, man."

Jackson slapped a hand to Ben's back. "I know. And she's going to need you. She's going to need all of us."

"I just hope I get the chance to give her what she needs."

"Don't think like that. Think about all the things we're going to do to Boyd and this Mars guy for messing with one of the Legends."

Ben took a deep breath and released it. "Damn straight."

CHAPTER TWENTY-FOUR

She knew it was coming. Even braced herself for it. But Paige still whimpered at the pain that radiated through her when the man's punch landed on her rib cage.

She had no idea how long the abuse had gone on. It felt like an eternity. Her abductor let her sleep a bit, so the drug he'd given her would wear off faster. As the effects lessened, her memory returned. She wished it hadn't. As much as she hated feeling confused, she hated knowing the truth even more.

He turned his back to her, and she thought he checked his watch. She'd noticed during one of the times he hit her that he sported a smart watch designed to receive messages as well as keep time. He glanced at it in between his monotonous tirades and hurtful attacks.

"Don't let me keep you if you have some place to be," she mumbled.

Her lip was split, and she tasted fresh blood on her tongue after she spoke. One of her eyes had already swollen shut. The man had ripped out her earrings while she'd been out of it. She wasn't sure if he'd done it because he knew they were transmitters or if he knew it would hurt her to rip them from her earlobes.

Her entire body felt broken. Her spirit felt fractured. She'd stopped hoping she'd be rescued. She'd stopped wishing Ben and his brothers would arrive in time to end the abuse. She'd stopped wishing the man would just kill her and be done with it.

She'd. Just. Stopped.

When the man turned back to her, he appeared amused, but despite the relaxed lines in his face, his eyes were the color of cold steel, hard and unforgiving.

"There's no other place I want to be, Paige. You are my priority. But our mutual friend has arrived. Now the fun can begin."

"You mean now you get to kill me?"

He laughed. It was a terrible sound. She squinted her uninjured eye at him, imagining the joy of smashing the laugh out of him with her baseball bat. If only she could get her hands on it or any weapon for that matter.

"I told you. I won't kill you. There is so much more we can do together. But our mutual friend…he's a different matter. When I'm through with you, he's going to get his turn. He's been waiting a long time."

"Let me guess. He's already killed my friend."

Paige's bravado slipped when she mentioned Ms. Miller. The man refused to tell her anything about her friend. Whenever she insisted he release her landlady, he only punched her and reminded her he was in control. She'd already figured out the man was working for Darius Boyd, and he toyed with her until Boyd showed up. She had no idea what kept Boyd, but it would make sense if he was taking care of Ms. Miller before coming to kill her.

"Stupid girl. We don't have your friend." The man's sneer was mocking. "We needed you to believe we did. You fell for it like a stupid bitch."

Paige felt like the man doused in her ice water. The shock was palpable, and her skin burned.

"You're lying."

"You're stalling."

His booted foot slammed down on her insole, and she screamed. He stepped away, checking his watch once more. She tried to catch her breath, but the pain was too much. She'd heard stories of people who became detached during times of abuse, numbing themselves to the effects. Perhaps her abductor was right. She was stupid because she hadn't been able to make that happen.

She could, however, believe the man about Ms. Miller. If he told the truth, then Ms. Miller was safe at home and untouched by the evil that targeted Paige. The idea that her friend was at the mercy of this man or Boyd terrified her, so she chose to believe he said, even if his intent was to mentally wound her and not reassure her.

Paige had been unable to study much of the room she was in. As far as she could see, the only thing in it was the chair she sat on. There were no windows. The area was small, giving the man room to pace, but little space for anything else. The light shining from the single bulb in the ceiling cast a pitiful yellow glow. It was enough to see by, but not enough to cast away the shadows.

The door to the room opened, jolting her. Paige tilted her head, so her one functioning eye could see a man striding through the opening. He paused to shake hands with her abductor.

"How is our guest doing, Mars?" Darius Boyd never looked her way, but he didn't have to. She never forgot anything about the man she knew as a murderer.

What the hell kind of name was Mars? She watched the two men interact with each other, talking too low for her to hear.

She didn't like the lighthearted, cool demeanor they showed, as if they conducted a business luncheon instead of plotting ways to hurt her. Knowing her torture would continue had tears welling in her eyes.

She had already pegged Mars as a calculating sadist. Now he was joined by a murderer, and Paige's time just ran out.

"Are we sure this is the place?"

Ben tightened his grip on his weapon as he peered through the trees to watch the building in the valley below. He could understand Jackson's skepticism. As far as hideouts go, the structure left a lot to be desired. Surrounded by high elevations, the targets would have difficulty defending the building against an attack. There weren't any visible security measures or any guards. The place looked deserted, save for the two vehicles parked out in the open in the front.

"She's here," Ben said. "I feel it. My gut senses trouble."

"Yeah," Jackson said. "Mine too."

The coms in their ears chirped. "We breaching or what?"

Jackson and Ben shared a pointed look. "We're breaching," Jackson told Easton. "Soft breach. In shifts. I don't know what we're walking into, so we have to be smart about it."

"Copy that," Easton acknowledged. "Luke and I will take the east side. Breaching in five."

"Copy," Jackson returned. "Ben and I will breach from the front. PJ?"

"We'll approach at the back. Remi, you and Ridge move in on the west side. Cutter, provide cover," PJ addressed his pilot, who set up a sniper perch with a clear view of the entry and exit points.

"Copy," Cutter repeated.

Jackson glanced at Ben, and he nodded to show his brother he was ready.

The teams moved in, traversing the hills with skillful precision. They seldom had reason to use the tactical moves they learned in the military, but when they did, their actions were second nature. Their eyes were sharp, their weapons at the ready.

The teams moved in. Ben and Jackson flanked the front door. The windows were boarded, so they had no view of the interior. Jackson used a hand signal to cue his brother. Ben tried the doorknob and found it locked. So much for a surprise entry.

Ben slammed his foot into a soft spot in the door, shattering the locking mechanism. Jackson was first through the door. He went left, and Ben went right.

"Front room clear," Jackson said a moment later.

The two kept moving with silent steps, as their team reported in.

"Clear."

"Back room clear."

"All's clear here."

The structure didn't have a lot of rooms or places for targets to hide. The place was quiet and empty, with dust coating the floor and windowsills indicating that no one had been there for a while. Very little time passed before the team regrouped in the front room.

With his gun secure in his hand, Ben paced liked a caged animal. He'd been certain they'd tracked down where Boyd and Mars held Paige. How could they have gotten this wrong?

"We saw Boyd come inside," Remi insisted, sounding as frustrated as Ben felt. "Where the hell could he have gone?"

Jackson frowned. "We search again. Check every room, every surface. Look for anything — and I mean *anything* — that looks out of place or could give us a clue as to where to find Boyd, Mars, or Paige. Luke, you, E, and PJ, check the perimeter for signs that they had a separate vehicle hidden nearby that they used to slip away. It doesn't make sense for them to leave their cars here and then vanish without some means of transport."

Ben pulled at the top of his bulletproof vest. The pressure in his chest built, and sweat beaded along his hairline. "E, you stay. I'll go with Luke and PJ. I need some air."

Jackson narrowed his eyes to study Ben. "Take a break. You look like shit."

"I'm good to keep searching. I just can't do it in here." Ben's eyes pleaded for his brother to understand.

Jackson nodded. "Yeah, okay. Easton, you search in here with us. Luke, PJ, and Ben, take the perimeter."

The group separated. Once outside, Ben breathed deep, letting the fresh air cleanse the disappointment from him. PJ and Luke started their search in the area closest to the structure and moving out to cover a greater distance. With his eyes adjusted to the limited visibility, Ben took a moment to study his surroundings. The bright moonlight illuminated the valley, so he had a better view of the perimeter than a nighttime search typically allowed.

They were surrounded by rolling hills sprinkled with trees and the one path that led to the front of the building. He closed his eyes and focused his mind. He was a Legend, just like his brothers. And just like his brothers, he brought his own strengths and skills to the job that the rest didn't have. He could play pretend. He could put himself in the mind of Paige's captors.

When he opened his eyes, he scanned his surroundings with a fresh perspective.

"Cutter, you still have eyes on the perimeter?"

"Roger that," the Atlas Security operative responded over the comm.

"Any evidence of a disturbance in the landscape? Something to indicate a possible underground bunker?"

"Standby."

Jackson stepped outside the building and stopped next to Ben. He didn't say anything, only watched and waited. Ben felt like an eternity slipped by before Cutter replied.

"I'll be damned. Less than a click to the west. Not sure if that's what you're talking about, but there's something there. I doubt you'll notice it from the ground. Head that way, and I'll tell you when to stop."

Jackson scowled. "An underground bunker is a stretch."

Ben shook his head. "This area is known for survivalist groups who don't exist without a bunker. In this area, it's the only way to stay hidden unless they go into the trees. I don't see that happening."

Jackson scanned the area, ever watchful. "No way to sneak up on them in a bunker."

"They're probably already waiting for us. We probably tripped some alarm when we breached," Ben reminded him.

"You would be right," Cutter interjected. "A little mole just stuck his head out of the hatch. Bet you a round at the bar that they're about to rabbit."

"Keep your eyes on them, Cutter. Remi and Ridge, secure the building and watch for unfriendlies. Everybody else, we're heading to the bunker. Going in hot."

Everyone moved on Jackson's command. Luke slapped Ben on the shoulder as he came up on his brother's right side.

"You ready to take down your girl's boogeyman?" Luke asked before they set off for the back of the property.

"I'm ready to get my girl. The boogeyman is up for grabs."

Luke grunted. "It'll be my pleasure to take that bastard out."

Ben focused on the terrain in front of them. He slowed his breathing, checked his weapon, and swiveled his head to check for any movement around them.

"ATV in the woods. Engine's warm. Site is clear."

PJ provided the update, and the back of Ben's neck started to itch. They were close.

"Target's running. No sign of hostage." Cutter's voice was low over the comms.

Despite his impulse to charge in and put an end to Paige's nightmare, Ben forced himself to remain calm and methodical. Her safety depended on all them being in control and smarter than her captors.

The bunker appeared in front of them. Cutter was right. They would have missed it if the hatch wasn't wide open like an X marking the spot.

"Rabbit is two clicks to your west," Cutter reported, and Jackson, PJ, and a couple of others from Atlas double-timed it in that direction through a thicket of trees.

"Follow my lead," Ben said just as two forms appeared from the bunker.

"Paige," he breathed, watching her move unsteadily on her feet. She looked ready to collapse, but she was alive.

His eyes narrowed, his gun poised, Ben positioned himself to take down the man who had taken his Paige.

Luke called out. "Stop! You're surrounded, so you might as well let her go."

Mars jerked Paige in front of him, his hold tight and awkward enough to make her cry out.

"He's got a blade," Cutter informed, his view sharper through the scope on his sniper rifle than what the team on the ground could make out.

"Stay back! I'll drop her right here!" Mars shouted at them.

"And we'll drop you," Easton retorted. "You're not getting away, man."

Paige struggled against him, but Mars only tightened his hold. He started backing away, holding Paige like a human shield.

"No shot," Cutter reported.

"What's the play, brother?" Easton asked Ben in a low voice.

Before Ben could answer, gunshots rang out. Mars broke out into a run, dragging Paige behind him. She stumbled to keep up, crying out in pain as they moved. She slowed him down, but he kept his grip on her and made sure she was positioned between him and their gunfire.

Ben began his pursuit, not wanting to lose sight of Paige. He doubted Mars would lead him on a merry chase without an end game in mind, and the man would sacrifice Paige without hesitation. Ben's speed and long strides closed the distance quickly.

Placing his gun in the side holster, he pitched himself forward. The bulk of his weight hit the man's waist. The force of the hit caused Mars to release Paige, and she collapsed to the ground with a scream that stopped Ben's heart.

His tackle sent him and Mars barreling across the rough terrain. Adrenaline kept Ben from feeling the hits to his body against the ground. He let go of his target when their momentum slowed. Ben propelled himself to his feet, squaring off against Mars.

Ben had some height and considerable muscle on the other man, but that didn't stop Mars from fighting to the bitter end. Pulling a gun from his waistband, Mars aimed at Ben's center mass.

The gunshots echoed through the valley in quick succession. One. Two. Three.

Then it was over.

CHAPTER TWENTY-FIVE

"No!" Paige screamed, trying to push herself up from the ground.

Her battered body wouldn't cooperate. Boyd and Mars' abuse did a number on her. She could barely move, and after running to keep up with Mars, her legs no longer supported her. But her body wasn't the only thing that couldn't keep up. Her mind also struggled.

Only minutes before, she had been in the middle of praying for death when a faint beep sounded in the room. Boyd froze with his fist in the air as he was about to bring it down on her head. Mars held his knife, waiting for his turn to cut her skin once more. With a curse, he moved away to check his phone. Then he swore again.

"We have company. They're at the primary location."

"Well, who the hell is it?" Boyd screamed, and Paige winced as the sound pierced her ears.

After several moments of staring at his phone, Mars scowled — the first sign of a loss of his self-control that Paige had seen.

"Tactical. SWAT maybe. With their arsenal and the way they move, they're heavily trained. We're vastly outnumbered."

"I thought you said no one could track us here."

Mars' cool façade slipped back into place. "You can stand here and yell at me. Or you can move. Either way, they're heading this way. They're trained to look for abnormalities in the terrain. They'll find us. We have to get out of here."

Boyd slammed his fist into the palm of his other hand as he released a frustrated shout. The noise startled Paige. Her body jerked in the seat, and she whimpered.

"Grab her. Let's go."

"Leave her," Mars countered. "She'll only slow us down. I can shoot her right now."

"No!" Boyd said. "Not until we figure out who and what she's told about me. No loose ends. You're on my payroll. I said grab her. We'll split up. You take her one way. I'll go another. We'll regroup once we get out of this mess."

Boyd started for the door, but Mars grabbed his arm and jerked him back. "I'm not a fool! You're not saddling me with your problem, so you can make your escape. I'm not going down for your mess."

Another beep had Mars staring at his phone again. Boyd took the opportunity to rush out the door before Mars stopped him. Mars shouted after him, but Boyd was already gone.

Mars whirled on her, wielding his knife. He roared and surged toward her. Paige had only seconds before he killed her with the knife. She squared her shoulders, forced her head up, and stared him down with her good eye.

"They know about you."

She held her breath, certain he would stab her despite what she said to stop him. Mars' chest heaved as he jerked to a stop in front of her. He dropped his arm, the hand grasping the knife at his side.

Relief washed over her, and she pushed herself to take advantage of the reprieve.

"The men who are here for me know all about you and what you've done. Kill me, and they'll come for you. Save me, and I'll help you take Boyd down for his betrayal."

"You think I need help for that?" Mars returned, his body barely holding his anger.

"I can keep you out of it. Just untie me and leave me here. You can escape, and I'll blame it all on Boyd."

Her breath caught when he approached, but he stepped behind her. She closed her eyes, certain he was about to slit her throat. She jerked when he cut her bindings and not her. She released a long breath as her arms fell to her side, numb and stiff.

Then he grabbed her arm and jerked her to her feet.

"Come on."

Paige swallowed the bile rising into her throat.

"I can't." She stumbled and almost dropped to the floor when her legs shook under her weight.

Mars crowded her space, glaring into her face. "You will, or I'll kill you."

"Leave me, please."

"Move!"

Paige had no idea how she managed to propel forward, but she did. Mars dragged her into a smaller area with a ladder leading up to a hatch. Realizing he held her in some sort of storm shelter, she tried to glance around her as they stepped at the top. It was still nighttime, and her unswollen eye struggled to adjust to the bright moonlight shining down on the unfamiliar area. All she discerned were shadows moving toward them.

It was Ben and his brothers. She didn't have to see clearly to know Ben had come for her.

"Move!" Mars shouted in her ear.

Her body wouldn't cooperate. He yanked on her violently, but her knees buckled. She heard someone shouting, but her pain roared in her ears. Mars' arm pressed to her chest like a vise, positioning her like a shield in front of him. He supported her, dragging her as they moved. Then he released her, only to grab her arm and pull her behind them in a run.

Paige had no idea how she managed to keep up with him when her body was shutting down. Tears streamed from her eyes, but she pushed on. She couldn't give up, not when Ben was so close.

Suddenly, she felt a *whoosh* of air blow past her. Mars released his hold, and she fell to the ground as Ben tackled Mars. Her arms were too weak to brace herself against the impact of hitting the ground. Her head bounced off the hard earth, and stars sparked behind her eyes.

She struggled to hold on to her consciousness, and she forced air in and out of her lungs. She rolled to her side with a moan. Her eye focused on the two shadowy figures ahead of her, but she identified Ben's form looming over Mars.

"Ben," she sighed, her voice barely audible.

Gunshots echoed around her. With wide-eyed terror, she watched Mars fall to the ground. And then Ben fell.

"No!"

Sobs wracked her body as her heart shattered. She closed her eyes, giving into the pain.

Someone suddenly dropped beside her, and unfamiliar hands lightly touched her face. Adrenaline mixed with panic surged within her. She fought against the person, knowing it was a losing battle with her weakened state. But she had to hold on. She had to get to Ben. He needed her.

"Paige. It's me. Easton. Ben's brother. It's okay. I've got you. You're safe. It's okay. It's Easton. Paige, you're safe."

Easton repeated the words a few times before they registered in her mind. Once she realized she was being held by a friend and not an enemy, she clung to him. Her tears clouded her limited vision.

"Ben. Oh, my God! You have to help him! You have to…"

"Paige, he's fine. He's fine. Look. He's up."

Easton pulled a cloth from a pocket and used it to clean her face. Then he gathered her gently in his arms and shifted her to gain a better view of the other men. Paige sagged against Easton in relief, fresh tears flowing. Ben stood, towering over Mars' defeated form crumpled to the ground. She wasn't sure if her abuser was dead or just severely wounded, but all that mattered was Ben was neither of those.

"Paige, honey, he's coming to you. We're getting you out of here and getting you some help. Do you understand what I'm telling you?"

She nodded once, unable to speak. Easton gently released her, and suddenly Ben was there. She didn't have to see him clearly to know it was him. Her battered body felt renewed, and she willed herself to sit up. Her hands framed his face, the feel of his rough, sweaty skin under her palms evidence that he was real. He was here. He came for her.

"Oh, baby, I'm so sorry," he breathed.

"Ms. Miller?" she whispered.

"Safe. They never kidnapped her. They just wanted you to believe they did."

She closed her eyes again and sagged against him. Ben supported her with his body and carefully wrapped her in his embrace. She placed a hand on his bicep, shocked to feel something wet and sticky clinging to her fingers. After battling through her confusion, she realized she wasn't the only one hurt.

"He shot you."

"It's nothing, Paige. I promise I'm fine. A lot better than him. Mars is dead."

Her breath hitched. "Boyd?"

"Not dead, but caught. You'll get your chance to tell the world what he's done and watch him be punished for it."

"But the evidence…" Her voice trailed off. Her head hurt too much for her to think, but she knew her situation wasn't over. Not yet.

"Baby, listen to me. I'm telling you all you have to worry about now is healing and spending the rest of your life with me."

"Okay," she breathed and collapsed against him.

Black spots swirled in front of her eyes. "Ben?"

"Yeah, baby."

"Did you…ask me to marry you?"

His chuckle rumbled through his chest, and she felt it soothe the broken pieces of her spirit.

"I think I told you that you were marrying me. I don't think I asked."

Her head swam. "I love you."

Then everything went black.

CHAPTER TWENTY-SIX

The news reporter detailed the story of the arrest of Darius Boyd, chronicling the relationship he had with Marty Warner, the plan he hatched to kill Warner and his family in cold blood, and the cover-up that followed. Though she lived most of it, Paige sat engrossed as the story unfolded. The news story concluded with an exclusive interview with Boyd's son Cassius. The presidential hopeful touted his father's innocence, passing the blame for the crimes onto Mars, who's background and true identity remained unknown.

Suddenly the screen went black, and Paige blinked in surprise. She reached for the remote control on the bedside table only to realize it wasn't there. Ben held it in his hand, his expression disapproving. But she didn't care. Seeing him in front of her, tall and powerful and sexy, was something she'd never tire of.

"I told you to stop watching the news coverage."

Her grin widened when he frowned at her. "I know, but I can't help it. I still can't believe Darius Boyd is going on trial for murder, and I'm free to be Paige Childers, living my life out in the open without fear."

His frown turned into a glare, and she laughed. "I mean, Paige Childers soon-to-be Weston."

His expression relaxed, and he placed a kiss to her cheek. "Ready to go home?"

Home. Paige's injuries required a lengthy hospital stay. In between surgeries, scans, IVs, and rest, she'd been questioned by law enforcement from so many agencies she stopped keeping up. No one would tell her any details of the investigation, and she realized she didn't care. She'd been concerned only with her healing and having Ben at her side.

He didn't disappoint. Once they patched up the superficial gunshot wound to his arm, he'd been with her nonstop. She'd had to enlist the help of his brothers in getting him to leave long enough to shower and change into fresh clothes, and that only happened because one of them stayed with her during the short time he was gone.

As a result, she enjoyed getting to know Jackson, Luke, and Easton. When she'd first come back to Fire Creek, she hadn't spent a lot of time with them while they were checking into her case. She'd spent more time with their wives, who had become close friends. But getting to know the boys and their unique personalities had given her insight into the man Ben was. He and his brothers shared a unique bond, and she was incredibly happy to see it.

She was most nervous to meet English and Becky because of how important they were to Ben. They were a huge influence on the man he was today, the man who had stolen her heart. But they accepted her, and she fell in love with them. Their family insisted there wasn't anything between English and Becky other than companionship, but Paige sensed there was something more. Paige even asked Becky about it once when they were left alone during a visit.

Becky had blushed and patted Paige's hand. "Honey, there's so much history between us, I don't know that we can ever have what you and Ben have or what the others share."

Paige had regarded her closely. "Ben loves the two of you so much. You've changed his life more than you know. It's natural that he wants the two of you to be happy. Now that I've met you both,

I can see why your family is so keen on seeing you and English together. May I ask what's holding you back?"

Becky shook her head. "You don't want to hear this. We should focus on you and our Ben."

"I understand if you don't want to talk about it, but I promise you, I'm willing to listen if you want to share."

It turns out Paige's encouragement was all Becky needed to open up. "For English, he's hung up on the age difference. And his first marriage didn't work out, so he's gun shy. Even after all these years."

"And for you?"

"I don't know. I don't want to ruin what we have by taking a chance and have it fail."

Paige had settled back against the pillows stacked at her back. "Fear can be a powerful and paralyzing thing. But from what Ben told me about you, I think you have the strength to kick fear in the ass."

Becky smiled and squeezed Paige's hand. "And you know what you speak because I hear you've done the same thing."

Paige had no idea if their talk helped Becky, but Paige felt a kinship with the woman. Ben's whole family accepted her, and for once in a long time, she was at peace.

"Paige, you okay?"

She shook off her wandering thoughts and realized she hadn't answered Ben's question.

"Yes, I'm fine. In fact, I'm more than ready to go home."

He bent down, and his lips pressed against hers in a lingering kiss. A thrill started at her toes and swirled up through her body, leaving her nerve endings tingling. He pulled away, and they shared a smile full of promise.

"I'll go check on the progress of your discharge. Be right back."

Ben left her alone, and she sighed. She could barely remember the last time she was this elated, and if her memory was correct, the same person was responsible for her happiness then as now. If someone had told her it was possible for a person to fall for her childhood best friend, she would have laughed, certain the idea was too fanciful to believe. But that was her reality. And it was perfect.

Paige ran a hand through her hair, her fingers snaring in the tangles. Frowning, she picked up the mirror a nurse left for her on the overbed table. She'd seen her reflection several times during her hospital stay, but this time, she saw herself as Ben did. Her hair was a mussed, tangled mess. Her skin was pale with colorful bruises marring her complexion. Her split lip was still a bit tender but was much better than when she first came in.

Compared to the rest of her body, her face fared better than she would have thought, considering how many times Mars had punched her. The cuts, bruises, and broken bones she suffered from on the rest of her body were taking longer to heal, but she was much better.

The door to her room opened, and she looked up with a smile, expecting to see Ben. The smile faded when Cassius Boyd stepped inside.

"What are you doing here?"

The charismatic man she'd seen on TV wasn't the man in front of her. Cassius looked crushed, his tailored suit replaced with jeans and a T-shirt. He held a pair of sunglasses and a ball cap in his hands. He didn't move from his place in front of the door. His eyes were fixed on his feet.

"I don't know."

His voice sounded like the man she'd heard speak, but he sounded lost. Desperate.

"You should go," she said with a little more force, straightening her posture to try and feel less vulnerable sitting in bed.

"I can't," he mumbled. Then he pierced her with dark, bloodshot eyes. "You have to take it back."

Paige stiffened. "Take what back?"

He held his hands out, palms up, as if begging her to listen to him. "Everything you told the police. You have to take it back. Tell them you lied. You're ruining everything."

"Seems like you should be saying that to your father."

He shook his head. "You don't know him. He's not the monster you told everyone he is. He gave me everything. How am I supposed to win this campaign without him coaching me? I've been preparing for this my entire life."

"Mr. Boyd — Cassius. It's not me you should be having this conversation with. I assure you, everything I said about your father is true."

"He's not a murderer!"

The man shouted, but Paige wasn't afraid of him. Though she wasn't sure why he'd come to visit her, she didn't believe he was here to hurt her.

"He is. I saw him. He shot Marty Warner to keep him from running against you and exposing your father for the man he really is."

Paige only repeated what the news media had pieced together. Cassius had heard it all, she was sure, but he was probably trying to reconcile it with what his father told him.

Cassius shook his head. "No! It's not possible."

"It is. Your father saw me there, and he came after me. He sent Mars after me too. They broke my wrist, broke my ribs, cut me, and terrorized me. I was forced to go into hiding. I gave up my business and my name. Everything that was important to me. He threatened people I care about. You love your father. You depend on him. I can see that, but I'm telling you that your faith in him is misplaced."

Cassius moved over to the window, and Paige almost felt sorry for him.

"Why? Why kill them? I could have won. I have what it takes to be the next president of the United States. He told me he believed in me. So why?"

"It was never about you."

Paige's head whipped back to the door, surprised that she hadn't heard Ben slip inside. He moved to place his body between her bed and Cassius, ready to strike out at the man if he posed a threat to her.

Cassius eyed Ben suspiciously. "Who are you?"

"Someone you don't want to mess with. My brothers and I took down your father. I'll take you down, too, if you make a wrong move."

"Don't threaten me!"

"It's not a threat. You should go."

"What did you mean that it was never about me?" Cassius demanded.

"Your father is only interested in power. The more power, the more money and influence, and the more he can have whatever he wants. This was never about you getting the presidency. This was about using you to get the power he craved and about protecting what he already had. You're a means to an end, Cassius."

Paige spoke softly. "He's right, Cassius. It's not me that ruined everything. That blame needs to be placed at your father's feet."

"What am I supposed to do with that?" Cassius' tone was a mixture of despair and frustration.

Paige reached for Ben's hand and clung to it. Ben moved his body to shield Paige from view.

"Other than leaving my fiancé alone for good? I don't give a damn what you do."

"Fiancé?" Cassius looked from Ben to her. "You're...getting married?"

"Yes," she said softly.

Cassius studied her, and she thought he looked...defeated. "It's all true, isn't it?"

"Yes," she repeated.

"I think I knew all along that something wasn't right. I didn't want to believe it. He's my father. I believed he sacrificed, so I could have the future I was destined to have. I can't believe it wasn't true. I just..."

Cassius held her gaze with his. "I think I had to face you and hear you say the words. I'm sorry to disturb you. I do wish you all the best. I hope...I hope you can put this all behind you."

Paige didn't respond. She wasn't sure she had the words to say that would bring him any peace. Ben shifted his weight to continue shielding her as Cassius crossed over to the door. He opened it and paused.

"I'm sorry to bother you." Then he was gone.

Ben rushed to the door, opened it, and checked to make sure Cassius was indeed gone. Then he was back at her side. He sat on her bed and touched her face gently, mindful of her still healing injuries.

"You all right? Did he touch you?"

She shook her head. "No. He just talked."

"Well, he's not going to come near you again. I'm getting you out of here, and you are coming back to my place to stay."

Paige smiled. "Sounds perfect. I have something I want to talk to you about once we get home."

He raised a quizzical brow. "Sounds interesting."

She sighed. "It is to me." She nibbled her bottom lip, not sure she could wait for them to get to his house before she told him what she'd been thinking about.

"Paige?" He drawled out her name, his voice rising in a question.

"I need your help. I want to find studio space and find some suitable equipment that I can afford. I want to open my photography business again."

"You sure?"

She could understand why he asked. It was her photography business that led her to witness a crime and live on the run under an alias.

"Yes, I'm sure. It's my gift. Even after all that happened, I can't turn my back on it. Not when I'm free to do what I love again."

He kissed her, the gesture brief but exciting. "Then we'll make it happen. Whatever it takes."

"I love you, Ben. More than I ever thought possible."

"I love you, too, baby. And I can't wait to show you just how much. Ready to get out of here?"

"Oh, yeah. Let's go home."

"Music to my ears," he said with a grin as the nurse stepped inside with her discharge papers.

EPILOGUE I

"You may now kiss your bride."

Ben wrapped his arms around Paige, swung her around, and tipped her back. He captured her lips in a kiss full of the hope, love, and passion he felt since getting to know her. The photographer they hired captured the moment, but Ben didn't care. He didn't need photographic proof to remember this day.

When he broke the kiss and swung her back to her feet upright, Paige's laugh rang out, startling the seagulls fishing nearby. The gentle waves provided a soothing cadence to their nuptials. They decided to be barefoot in the sand as they exchanged their vows in front of the minister. Ben's tan linen pants and matching open neck shirt were lightweight enough to be perfect for the May evening, but Paige stole the show in her flowy dress with tiered skirt, spaghetti straps and deep vee neckline.

"Congratulations, Mr. and Mrs. Weston," the officiant said.

Ben and Paige thanked the man for leading their sunset ceremony. They accept congratulations from the destination wedding director and the photographer, who also served as witnesses to the wedding. And then the newlyweds were alone.

"May I have this dance, Mrs. Weston?" Ben extended a hand and formally bowed in front of her.

She giggled. "We don't have any music."

He took her hand and twirled her into his arms. "We don't need any."

They began to sway to the sound of the waves, the sunset casting a soft glow around them. Ben held her gaze, unable to look away.

"You're breathtaking."

Her smile was radiant. "I must be because you cried when I walked down the beach toward you."

"Happy tears, baby. Most definitely, happy tears."

She caressed his cheek. "No more tears. Only smiles. We've come too far for anything else."

They had far to go, but Ben wouldn't disagree with her. She made him proud when she testified at Darius Boyd's arraignment, and the man was held without bond for murder, extortion, and fraud. Once Atlas Security turned over the evidence they uncovered, Boyd's fate was sealed even without Paige's eyewitness testimony. Cassius withdrew his campaign for president, and the Boyd family hid from society, not even appearing in court.

Ben had been cleared of any wrongdoing in Mars' death. The man's true identity remained a mystery, but that was a mystery left to be unraveled by law enforcement.

Paige moved in with him and started plans to get her photography business up and going. So far, she'd found several satisfied customers to keep her out of the red, but she was far from achieving the success she enjoyed before she had to go into hiding.

Because of the court proceedings, building her business and settling back into her life, Paige had little time to focus on wedding planning. When she asked Ben about eloping, he'd readily agreed because all that mattered to him was being married to the love of his life. When they asked his family if they would be upset with the elopement, they insisted they supported the couple no matter what type of wedding they decided to have.

Paige and Ben wanted the wedding to be just the two of them.

With the choice made, they secured their marriage license, picked a weekend, and headed to Hawaii for their dream ceremony.

"You know what I'm thinking, Mrs. Weston?"

"That you're hungry? Because I know I'm starving. I've been too nervous to eat much today. I've gotten my appetite back all of a sudden."

He kissed her, never tiring of the taste of her lips. "I'm hungry all right. I just don't have food on my mind."

Her eyes brightened with a mixture of love and desire. "Hmm. I'm not thinking of food now either."

Their bungalow was up the beach nearby, and with their hands linked, the couple hurried toward their home away from home. Once inside, Ben cradled her face, memorizing each lovely feature.

"I love you, Paige Weston. I think I fell in love with you that day on the playground when you stood up for the scrawny little boy with a stutter."

Her eyes glistened with unshed tears. "You mean you didn't fall in love with me when I broke your nose?"

He barked out a chuckle that quickly grew into a belly laugh. She joined in, and Ben marveled at how good it felt to laugh with her. He pulled her closer and placed a lingering kiss on her lips. Her fingers were on the buttons of his shirt, and soon they were frantically removing any barriers preventing their bodies from touching.

His hands and his lips caressed her neck, her breasts, her stomach, and her core until she writhed underneath him. She touched his hair, his biceps, his six-pack, and his ass as she pushed him inside her. They carried each other to the height of passion, falling over the cliff of their climax together. Coming down from the high, they cradled each other in a tangle of limbs.

"Happy, Mrs. Weston?" He pressed his lips to her hair.

"More than I thought possible."

"That's exactly how I feel."

She propped her head up with her hand and smiled at him. "And we still have the rest of our lives to make each other even happier."

"I can't wait, baby."

She sighed and cuddled next to his side. "Me either."

EPILOGUE II

Two years later...

Reagan turned to the side, studying her profile critically. Preoccupied with her growing waistline, she didn't notice Jackson coming into the bedroom until his arms encircled her waist.

"I think I'm gaining more weight with this pregnancy than I did with Jax," she grumbled.

His response was a slow smile as he reached up to cup her fuller breasts. "I'm not complaining."

She rolled her eyes. "I'm serious, Jackson. I'm having to wear maternity clothes sooner this time. By the time I deliver, you'll have to roll me to the hospital because I won't fit in the car."

He turned her around and drew her close. Their kiss was slow and heated. He raised his head to stare into her dark eyes. "Ray, you're beautiful. Our baby will be beautiful. I would appreciate it if you stopped all the negative talk about my wife."

Sighing, she closed her eyes as if to reset her attitude. When she opened them, she placed her hands on her husband's chest and smiled. "I'm sorry. You're right. Our baby boy will be amazing. I can't wait to meet him and watch Jax be the best big brother. Maybe by the time he arrives, we'll have a name for him."

"I've been thinking about that, and I have an idea. What do you think of Jett?"

She was silent, and he could tell she was considering his suggestion. "I love it. It's perfect. How did you come up with it?"

Jackson scowled. "I hate to admit it, but Easton picked it. But I like it too. It's cool."

"What do you think about Jett Adam Moore?"

Jackson blinked. "Really? After all this time trying to decide, did we come up with a name just like that?"

Reagan giggled. "I think so."

"Mom!" Jax's voice rang out from his room, and Reagan placed her head against her husband's chest.

"Duty calls."

Jackson dropped a kiss to her hair. "I've got to get to the bar. You go take care of whatever crisis our son is having. Then tonight, we celebrate finding a name for our baby boy."

"Sounds like a plan."

Luke knew something was up the moment he stepped into his home. The lighting was dim, soft music played, and rich aromas wafted from the kitchen, smelling suspiciously like his favorite meal.

"Mel?"

He listened for his wife, and when he didn't hear her, he started searching. First the kitchen, then the back patio. Her home office. The bathroom and finally their bedroom. She stood there, a silky slip of a dress draping enticingly over the curves of her body. Her thick curls spilled over her shoulders. Her teeth worried her bottom lip.

He closed the distance between them. His thumb pulled her lip free, and he lightly kissed her.

"Hi."

She smiled sweetly. "Hi. I'm glad you're home."

"If I'd known you were waiting for me looking like sin in a dress, I'd have been here sooner."

He reached for her, but she stepped out of his embrace. "I have a surprise for you."

She placed a blank envelope in his hand, and he eyed it like it might explode.

"Open it, Luke."

He ripped the envelope and withdrew a piece of paper. He read the words twice before their meaning registered. Raising his head, he met his wife's nervous stare with a wide smile.

"You're pregnant?"

"Yes. Nine weeks."

Luke let out a loud *whoop* as he lifted Melody off her feet and swung her around. When he sat her back down, he kissed her soundly, his hand spanning over her abdomen.

"How are you feeling? You okay?"

Melody grinned. "I'm fine. Tired and a bit nauseous. The doctor said that's normal. Everything with the baby checked out. Little baby Meade is healthy and growing."

"Damn. You sure you want to have a baby with me? I'm not exactly father of the year material, you know."

Melody's hands framed his face. "You are a great man. You are a wonderful husband. I have no doubt you will be an amazing father. So you put those doubts out of your head right now. They have no business ruining our celebration."

"Our celebration?"

"Yeah. I thought we'd have a nice salad, juicy steak, and baked potato. And then for dessert, you get me."

Her smile was seductive, and her body rubbed against him, making his cock sit up and take notice.

Luke settled his hands on her hips. "I think I want my dessert first."

"Our dinner will get cold," she warned him.

"So I'll eat a cold steak. It will be worth it."

Melody smiled as she shared a long, passionate kiss with her husband.

Easton stepped into the house with Dylan riding piggyback. They were met by the loud wailing of two very unhappy, very hungry baby girls.

"Uh, oh. Sounds like Momma needs some help."

He set Dylan on his feet with orders to wash up. Then he followed the sound of his daughters' crying to the nursery. Bailee was bent over the changing table, using wipes to clean a messy Abby Lynn. Easton stopped beside a baby bed to lift a sobbing Bella Rose into his arms, blowing a raspberry to her round cheek. She laughed through her tears.

Bailee spared him a grateful glance. "Thanks. The twins have been cranky all day. I think they're teething."

Lightly bouncing his daughter to soothe her, he walked over to kiss his wife's cheek. She smelled of baby formula with spit-up staining her shirt, and she was still the prettiest, fiercest woman he'd ever seen.

"What can I do to help?"

"You're doing it," she said with a tired smile. "How was Dylan's T-ball practice?"

"He had a blast. He loved using his new glove, and he made friends with one of the other boys. He said the kid goes to his school, but they aren't in the same class. Scotty something."

"Oh, yeah. Scotty Beason. I know his mom, Lydia. She's a teller at the bank. Very nice, and Scotty seems like a good kid."

Bailee lifted Abby Lynn and stood facing her husband. The girls were starting to calm down now that they were being held. They were going through a clingy phase, which seemed doubly hard with twins. Easton dropped another kiss to his wife's cheek.

"Tough day?"

"Long day," she clarified. "I was just about to start dinner when Abby Lynn let me know she needed a diaper change. Once she started crying, Bella Rose started in too. Solidarity and all that."

Easton chuckled. "Want me to have a pizza delivered for dinner?"

Bailee sighed. "That sounds perfect."

"And I'll put the kids to bed tonight, so you can rest and relax the rest of the evening."

Her smile sparkled in her eyes. "And that's why I love you so much."

Shifting Bella Rose to his hip, he draped an arm around Bailee's shoulders. "I love you, too, Bailee Anne. More than you'll ever know."

Paige snuggled into Ben's side, staring at the sonogram picture in her hand. Her head rested against his chest, and a smile crossed her lips when she thought of their sweet baby growing inside her, a testament to how much their love for each other had grown.

"When should be tell everyone?"

"We're getting together with Gish and Becky on Saturday. We can tell everybody then if you want."

"Think they'll be excited?"

"In case you haven't noticed, our family has become baby crazy lately."

Paige chuckled. "I've noticed. But do you think they'll be surprised that we're having a girl?"

"I think they'll be ecstatic. You sound nervous though."

Paige shook her head. "No, not nervous. A little anxious. Excited. Curious. I can't help but wonder what she'll be like. I hope she has your eyes."

"Nope. She's going to be blond with blue-gray eyes, just like her beautiful momma."

"It doesn't matter, does it? As long as she's healthy, that's all that matters."

Ben brushed his lips against her hair. "You're right."

They settled in to watch a streaming movie on the smart TV, but after a few moments, Paige looked up at her husband. "Ben? Do you think we could ask Wally and Mona to be our daughter's godparents?"

The couple visited their friends in Ivy Springs often. Paige owed them and the town so much. They'd given her refuge when she needed it, and the town was where she reconnected with Ben.

"I think that's an excellent idea."

Paige smiled. Snuggling closer to Ben's side, she went back to studying the sonogram picture, feeling contentment spreading though her chest. Life with Ben had been ideal, and the things in her life that had once been painful now brought her joy. With a daughter on the way, she was excited to see what the future held for them.

"When should we tell them?"

"I'll call them all right now if you want. I don't know how to do that group calling thing on my phone, but I think I could figure out. I used to work for the CIA for Christ's sake."

Becky Lathan laughed as she snuggled close to English Barlowe's side. A bird chirped outside their bedroom window, and an owl hooted in response. English drew circles on her arm with his finger, his light touch giving her goosebumps.

"Saturday. When we're all together. What do you think they'll say?"

"That it's about damn time."

Becky had to agree. After years of imagining a life with English, she was living her dream. Seeing the boys find true love with four phenomenal women inspired her. They'd overcome dangerous and life-changing circumstances to find happiness. It was enough to make Becky wonder why she was afraid to take a chance with English. So she cornered him one evening at the bar and told him as much.

He responded by kissing her. Then he told her she was staying at his place that night, and they would make their relationship official. They'd been together every day since, keeping it a secret from their kids until they knew it was going to last. Now that English was living with her, it was time to let their family know about their decision to be together.

"I don't know. I was planning to talk to the boys about something else on Saturday while they were here," English said.

"Oh? Sounds serious."

He didn't respond immediately, and Becky waited, knowing he'd tell her when he was ready.

"The boys are married and starting families of their own. I'm wondering if maybe we should cut back on their work as Legends. The cases can be dangerous, so it makes sense for them to slow down and protect themselves. They have people depending on them to be around for a long time."

Becky raised up in surprised. "Really? You think so? I'm not sure I like the idea of this world without the Legends helping those who need it. They wouldn't have the families they have now without their work. I wouldn't be here without your work. I understand why you think it might be time. It's just hard to imagine."

English released a long breath. "Maybe you're right. The boys haven't mentioned anything about stepping back. If the girls wanted them out of harm's way, they'd say so. Maybe I shouldn't say anything. I guess I'm just nervous about something happening now that they have everything they deserve."

"They are living out their calling. They're smart, and you've taught them how to be careful, especially now that there is more at stake. They'll know when the time is right for them to step back, and you can be there to tell them it's okay. That their work as Legends is done, and they can step back knowing they've changed lives for the better. But they'll be the ones to decide."

"You've always understood that, haven't you? Their need to help people who need it. Not many people do."

"As someone who benefited from the original Legend's protection, yes, I can understand it. And I'm proud of those boys. Folks in this town thought they would grow up to be troublemakers and good-for-nothings. But they are bright, handsome, caring men who make a difference. I'm glad I had a ring-side seat to see it happen."

English kissed her. "For the life of me, I do not understand why you want to be with the likes of me or why you've hung around all these years. You've had so many chances to live a completely different life, but you stayed."

"Because you are an amazing man, English Barlowe."

He shook his head. "I'm just a man, Becky. An old one at that."

"Old or not, you're mine. And I love you."

He smiled, his blue eyes shining. "I love you too, Becky. I'm sorry I didn't tell you sooner, but I swear to you that I'll say it every day until I draw my last breath."

"Sounds like a long, perfect life to me."

AUTHOR'S NOTE

I really hope you enjoyed Ben and Paige's story. Knowing this was going to be the last book in this series, I decided I wanted it to be full of twists and turns. I wanted it to be epic — at least by my standards.

The case involving the suspected child abuse that turns out to be a kidnapping was originally meant to be Easton's case. I wrote several chapters of this for Easton and quickly got frustrated because the story never seemed to come together the way I wanted. So I abandoned that idea and took Easton's story in a different direction.

I revisited that subplot with Ben, and after a few tweaks here and there, it seemed to work well.

The part of this story where Ben and Paige knew each other as children and reconnected as adults was my intention for them all along. My imagination has been toying with that storyline for a while, and I loved how it came full circle.

Lastly, I had to include a happily-ever-after for English and Becky. I've been asked a few times if they were going to get their own story. It was never in the plans to write their story. When I started this series, I never intended them to be a couple. But as the series progressed, I realized they needed a resolution as any good romance story delivers. They worked out their feelings for each other quietly in the background with hints being revealed as the others in their lives discovered them.

If you are one of the readers who hoped for more with English and Becky, I'm sorry if you're disappointed. The fact is that I have to be inspired to create a story before I can write it, and a full story for English and Becky never came to mind. I believe these characters were content to stay in the background, and I had no trouble with that.

Thank you for joining me on this author journey. I can't believe I now have two complete book series under my belt. My thirteen-year-old self is amazed. My much older self is doing a happy dance while already thinking of the next book.

If you enjoyed this final book in the Legends of Fire Creek series or any of my books for that matter, please consider leaving a review on <u>Amazon</u>, <u>Goodreads,</u> and/or <u>Bookbub</u>. Reviews are so important to indie authors, so I hope you take the time to do this, even if it's just a few words. They mean so much.

You can also support me by sharing my books with others you know who will enjoy them, by following me on social media, by liking and commenting on my posts, and by requesting local libraries and bookstores to carry my books. Your support means more than I can ever put into words (and I'm never at a loss for words).

Take care. Happy reading. And be on the lookout for my new projects in the works. I'm hoping to introduce the first of those very soon.

ABOUT THE AUTHOR

Shelley Justice is a Southern belle who lives with her husband and her Lab mix fur baby in northern Alabama. She is a mom to two grown daughters, one of whom just got engaged to the love of her life. Shelley's fascination with the written word inspired her to start writing when she was thirteen years old, and she's been living in her imagination and crafting stories ever since. You are welcome to check out her website at *www.shelleyjustice.com*.

ACKNOWLEDGMENTS

For everyone who had a hand in getting this book ready to be in the hands of readers — thank you! I couldn't do this without you! My creative team is the best: Christopher John with CJC Photography, Clarise Tan with CT Cover Creations, my author bestie Emily Gray for always being my sounding board and encourager, and my real life bestie, Christie, for all the things.

Thank you to all of the great author/reader event coordinators who give me an opportunity to share my books and connect with readers. I've been blessed to be a part of some amazing events. When many authors have encountered problems, I have had wonderful experiences.

Thank you to my sweet family for all the ways you support my love for writing.

To my readers, thank you for buying my books. Thank you for recommending them. Thank you for the reviews and the encouragement. Thank you for always asking when the next one is coming because you motivate me to get going. You are the best!

MORE FROM THIS AUTHOR

Meet the
LEGENDS OF FIRE CREEK

They were once wayward boys until they were taken under the wing of the original Legend. They grew under his tutelage to become vigilantes who look after those who aren't able to help themselves. They are loners thrown together in an unconventional family, living with secrets which shaped them into the men they've become. None of them know the meaning of the word normal, but they've known no other way — until they meet the women who show them what it means to be loved and accepted for who they are.

LEGENDS: JACKSON
Book One

LEGENDS: LUKE
Book Two

LEGENDS: EASTON
Book Three

LEGENDS: BEN
Book Four

Read more from Author
SHELLEY JUSTICE
KNIGHTS OF KSI SERIES

Available on Amazon
Read for Free with Kindle Unlimited

KNIGHT'S HAVEN
Book One

KNIGHT'S RESCUE
Book Two

KNIGHT'S TEMPTATION
Book Three

KNIGHT'S JOURNEY
Book Four

KNIGHT'S HOLIDAY
Book Five

KNIGHT'S DESIRE
Book Six

KNIGHT'S FALL
Book Seven

KNIGHT'S SEDUCTION
Book Eight

KNIGHT'S HONOR
Book Nine

COMING SOON

The Wilder Sisters Trilogy

Tentative Release: 2026

Zane Wilder had his story told in *Knight's Journey*, Book Four in the popular Knights of KSI series. Now it's time for his sisters to step into the spotlight, finding love with some familiar faces around Grayson Cove.

As the oldest of the Wilder siblings, **Zoe** has always been the protector, looking out for everyone else while her needs took a backseat. Her boyfriend considered that her second biggest flaw. Her first? Her generous curves that kept her body from fitting into a size two. But the boyfriend is out of the picture, and the time has come for Zoe to make herself a priority. Some people have a bucket list. Zoe has a self-improvement list. But when she meets a man who sees her flaws as reasons to fall in love with her, can she embrace her uniqueness and find the happiness she deserves before it's taken away? Find out in **Book One of the Wilder Sisters Trilogy, WILD HEART.**

Zaida has always been a tomboy at heart. Chasing after her brother, who is also her best friend, she preferred fishing and football to flirting and fairy tales. Now that Zane found his true love, Zaida thinks maybe she should give romance a try. Unfortunately instead of a prince, she finds a lot of frogs who want to change her instead of embracing her wild ways. Determined to prove to herself that she can find happiness on her own, she sets out on an adventure that leads her straight into danger. Her only hope lies with the man who knows how to push all her buttons. Mr. All Wrong for Her is the one her heart — and her life—needs the most. Discover Zaida's story in **Book Two, WILD FIRE.**

Zaylee's brother is her hero, and no other man has ever measured up to the standard Zane set for what a man and a husband should be. Everyone assumes that quiet and timid Zaylee wants a love that's safe and expected. Only Zaylee knows what her heart yearns for — a love that's exciting, a man who curls her toes, and a life full of the unexpected. Her life may be boring now, but her future won't be. Not if she finds the right match. But outside appearances can be deceiving, and when Zaylee finds the kind of excitement that might mean her death, it's an unlikely hero who shows her what truly matters. The **third and final book in the trilogy, WILD CARD**, will leave you wanting more.

Atlas Security

Tentative Release: 2027

You met them in the Legends of Fire Creek. Fall in love with them in a new series featuring the men and women of Atlas Security. They've worked in the background supporting the Legends. Now Alex, Drake, PJ, Remi, Ridge, Cutter, and the rest will step into the spotlight. The result is all the action, adventure, and romance your own heart craves.